THE COLUMNIST
MURDER

THE COLUMNIST
MURDER

Lawrence Saunders

COACHWHIP PUBLICATIONS
GREENVILLE, OHIO

The author wishes to make it plain to the reader that all the events in this tale are imaginary and all the characters fictitious. He is deeply grateful to his wife, Clare Ogden Davis, for the plot of the piece.

The Columnist Murder, by Lawrence Saunders
© 2025 Coachwhip Publications edition
Introduction: © 2025 Curtis Evans

First published 1931
John Burton Davis, 1893-1970
Clare Ogden Davis, 1892-1970
CoachwhipBooks.com

ISBN 1-61646-601-4
ISBN-13 978-1-61646-601-5

INTRODUCTION
Curtis Evans

Lawrence Saunders was the author of three American detective novels in the early Thirties: *Smoke Screen* (1930), *The Columnist Murder* (1931) and *Devil's Den* (1933). In reality the pseudonymous name of Lawrence Saunders—recalling Gwen Bristow and Bruce Manning, authors, right around the same time, of *The Invisible Host* and three other mysteries—hid a married pair of journalists, John Burton Davis and Clare Ogden Davis. Constantly coming face to face with crime in their journalistic careers, reporters like Bristow and Manning and the Davises not unnaturally decided to try their hands at fictional murder.

John Burton Davis was born in Perryville, Missouri, in 1893 to newspaper editor John Brooks Davis and his wife Laurette Saunders Davis, whose maiden name Saunders provided half of the inspiration for "Lawrence Saunders." (The Lawrence half came from the maiden surname of Clare Ogden's mother.) Burt entered the school of journalism at the University of Missouri in 1913, but withdrew after only a year to convalesce from illness at balmy Brownsville, Texas. So did the young man inadvertently turn the key in the lock of the door to his life's great adventure.

In 1915 the *Brownsville Daily Herald* put Burt on its news staff and in 1916-17 the enterprising, bilingual cub

CLARE OGDEN DAVIS

reporter inveigled himself into serving as an interpreter with General Pershing's punitive Mexican expedition against the notorious revolutionary Pancho Villa. While the Great War, which soon ensnared the United States, continued to rage overseas in Europe, Burt worked at the *Houston Post* and lodged at the local YMCA. His draft registration card describes him as tall, of medium weight, with brown eyes and black hair.

1920 found Burt in Fort Worth employed with the *Record*, where he met spunky, redheaded "girl reporter" Clare Ogden, who worked in the Fort Worth office of the Dallas *Morning News* and was reputedly the first woman in Texas ever to cover police assignments for a newspaper. In classic film fashion Clare professed to loathe the tall, brash, black-haired newsman at first sight, later declaring of their initial meeting: "I saw him and asked somebody who is that scarecrow who thought he was a little tin god." Thirteen days later in full romcom fashion the little tin god proposed marriage to the pioneering newswoman and she accepted.

The Davis marriage, which never produced any children, was not without bumps in the road, however. "Surely we've had fights," Clare reflected in 1932, when the pair were promoting *Six Weeks*, a mainstream Reno divorce novel. "We've been near to divorce [ourselves] at least twice. . . . I think perhaps the thing that holds us together is the fact that neither has a better friend than the other."

The union of these two best friends, who after some years in New York (see below) returned to live in Austin, Texas, after World War Two, endured for a half-century. Clare suffered a debilitating stroke in 1965, forcing her to retire from the column in the Austin *American*, "In My Texas Garden," which she had written since 1951. Burt loyally kept it up himself for a year, pending Clare's promised return, but she never made it back. He died from

TWO GARDENERS—When Former Governor Miriam A. Ferguson, right, and her former press secretary, Clare Ogden Davis, new resi- dent of Austin, visited for the first time in many years, they talked of flowers and herbs and how to make a garden grow. (Staff Photo by Bill Monroe.)

1951

cancer at the age of seventy-six in April 1970 and Clare, still bedridden, finally passed away a month after her husband at the age of seventy-seven. It was a sad end to two distinguished and dynamic careers.

Clare Ogden had been born near Waco, Texas in 1892 to a pair of prosperous ranchers. She graduated in 1913 from Baylor College at Belton, a private Christian women's university (now the University of Mary Hardin-Baylor) and taught high school history for several years before finally landing her first newspaper job. After her marriage to Burt, the couple resided in Texas for several more years, working at papers in Fort Worth, Dallas, Houston, and San Antonio. Between 1923 and 1925 Clare lived apart from Burt in Europe, reporting for Texas papers on international events. It was said she was the last reporter to interview novelist Joseph Conrad before his death.

In 1925 Clare returned to Texas to become press secretary for Miriam A. (Ma) Ferguson, Texas' controversial first woman governor. Meanwhile Burt that same year was hired by the New York *Morning Herald* to serve as the paper's drama editor and critic and work as a press agent for showman Florenz Ziegfeld of Ziegfeld Follies fame. Miriam left her press secretary post to join him in 1926, three years later drawing on her experiences with Ma Ferguson to publish a novel, *The Woman of It*, about—surprise—a woman governor of a southern state.

Having caught the fiction bug, Clare collaborated with John over the next four years on four novels, three of which were mysteries, which were then enjoying a terrific vogue in the United States, with S. S. Van Dine's critically lauded Philo Vance puzzlers ascending high up on the bestseller charts, inspiring hosts of hopeful imitators. Clare and John were no slavish followers of the Great Detective school of mystery, however. To the contrary, their mysteries were models of what was then deemed real-ism, with protagonists who are ordinary onlookers as well as amateur sleuths, helping the police solve the crimes but being by no means showoff, tediously declamatory geniuses like hoity-toity Philo Vance and Lord Peter Wimsey. Clearly the couple brought their own extensive professional portfolios to bear on their crime writing.

In *Smoke Screen*, the debut Lawrence Saunders detective novel, the protagonist surely not altogether coincidentally is a daring woman newspaper reporter in Houston, Texas. A "keen-witted society girl" bored with teas and dances who fervently desires to be taken seriously at the male-dominated *Pioneer*, Sally Lomax is returning from a roadhouse early one morning with Johnny Rorke, hotshot star of the staff, when a fire engine shrieks by them. Sally insists to the jaded Johnny that they pursue the vehicle. "Sally always followed fire engines," we are told, hoping to find a hot story. This time the one she and Johnny discover is a five-alarm scorcher!

In the smoldering remains of a partially burnt bungalow are found the bodies of an old man and a pretty young woman—and it soon becomes apparent, in part due to Sally's pertinacious on-the-spot investigating, that the fire was deliberately set and its victims actually murdered. Sally has finally found her big story and no one is going to deflect "Miss Sherlock" from chasing it, no matter how much the danger heats up! At first she is treated patronizingly by her colleagues, but eventually her editor, Andy Hunt, is upbraiding himself for his male chauvinism: "By God, he had taken this girl for a society dumb-bell! Wanted to fire her! Suppose he had! Good Lord!"

Granted, Sally enjoys every social advantage in life—she has not only a devoted black maid, Lulu, but her brother, Dick, happens to be Houston's DA—but she is not afraid to get her dainty hands dirty. And dirty is just what this double murder case turns out to be before truth eventually is outed. "[T]hat was the way the game was played," thinks Sally unsentimentally when it is all over. "She had been a sneak and an eavesdropper and felt proud of herself."

One suspects that *Smoke Screen* was written mostly by Clare and that the follow-up Lawrence Saunders mystery, *The Columnist Murder*, came more from Burt's hand. In this book a corpse is discovered shot in a phone booth during the debut performance of a hit show at the New Netherland Theater on Broadway. The victim is newspaper society gossip columnist Tommy Twitchell, whom the authors obviously based upon real-life society gossip columnist Walter Winchell (1897-1972), who a couple years earlier in 1929, while working at the *New York Daily Mirror*, had inaugurated the country's first syndicated gossip column, *On Broadway*.

Tommy Twitchell's dead body is discovered by youthful native Norwegian Nels Lundberg, the house fireman on duty at the theater, whom the authors describe as "[t]wenty-five, blond, burly and handsome" and one reviewer praised for his "Scandinavian phlegm." Nels fervently desires to become a cop and manages to tag along for the police investigation into Tommy's murder, which concludes about eight hours later. Nels makes some important discoveries himself, like the torn copy of Tommy's latest innuendo-laden column (facsimile copies of which were included in the original hardcover edition of the detective novel). Can the motive for Tommy's murder be found in a fatal, final divulgement of tittle-tattle from the gossip writer?

The authors dedicated *The Columnist Murder* to Walter Winchell, who certainly had nothing to take umbrage with in the book concerning tittle-tattle about himself.

ON BROADWAY *By* WALTER WINCHELL

A Columnist's Sec'y Jots Down a Few Notes

Dear W. W.: I saw a sample jacket of "The Columnist Murder," the crime novel which Farrar-Rinehart plan to present in July...It is a striking cover for a book, revealing a blood-stained finger pointing to an item such as appears in your quidnunc col'm...A blurb states: "A gossip item looked harmless, but three gruesome deaths followed!"...Have yourself a shiver...They say, however, that Lawrence Saunders (Burton Davis to you!) has done a thrilling job of it, but so far as I am concerned he will go down in literary history as being another novelist who turned yellow when it came to mentioning your name, when he meant you...

He calls his central character "Tommy Twitchell" . . . How subtle! . . .At any rate, this is the book in which you are killed while in a phone booth during a performance of the "Follies" . . . By the way, Time, the magazine, phoned . . . Wanted to know if the time had not expired on the statement of six months ago in Zit's Weekly that you would be bumped off within six months . . . As soon as you come in rush upstairs to Mr. K . . . What have you done now?

1931

Although by the 1960s Winchell—who had distinguished himself in the McCarthyite Fifties as a notorious McCarthyite redbaiter and cruelly wanton career destroyer—was generally despised, at the inception of his career in the early Thirties he was tolerated rather more as a playful scamp. I happen to have a copy of the novel that contains an inscription from Burt and Clare to Robert John Conway, *who helped a lot.* Robert John Conway (1899-1972) was a nationally prominent journalist who had covered the infamous Hall-Mills and Snyder-Gray murder trials in 1926 and 1927 respectively. He would go on to receive a nomination for a Pulitzer Prize in 1935 for his coverage of the Bruno Hauptman Lindbergh baby kidnapping trial.

In 1932 Burton and Clare Ogden Davis published a final detective novel, *Devil's Den*, which they set in the Devil's Den Preserve, the largest natural park in southwestern Connecticut and one of the biggest in the metropolitan New York area. Nels Lundberg, now a cop, is again on a case in this, the last and by far the longest of the Lawrence Saunders detective novels. Hopefully it too will be reprinted someday.

To Walter Winchell

"Integer vitae, scelerisque purus non eget mauris iac-
ulis neque arcu nec venenatis gravida saggittis . . ."
—Quintus Horatius Flaccus Carminum,
Book I, Ode 22.

(The man of pure and upright life has
naught to fear from the Tabloid papers.)

1

"Curtain going up!"

Through the smoke and the din the doormen were barking to herd the sheep with the golden fleece back into their stalls for the second act of *Rebel Rose*.

"Curtain going up!"

A thousand men and women in evening dress were jammed in like subway strap-hangers, from the vestibule doors that shut off the smoky, perfumed heat of the lobby from the wintry, wind-swept dazzle of Forty-second Street, back through the long, wide corridor that ran halfway through the block to the auditorium doors. In the promenade at the rear of the orchestra floor, upstairs in the balcony lounge and downstairs in the smoking room they were standing, too, back to back, elbow to elbow, sables to broadcloth, starched shirt to bare bosom, smoking, laughing, staring, preening, making small talk and big talk, as elaborately at ease as extras in a society film. This was the audience's part of the show. To swarm like bees between the acts, to see and be seen by each other, and only incidentally to see the premiere of Karyl Wilde's annual girl-and-music masterpiece, some had paid as much as a hundred dollars for a ticket.

"Curtain going up! Please resume your seats!"

The burly carriage caller in a green greatcoat was opening the plate-glass outer doors. The icy air, pouring in, began to carry the reluctant crowd with it. On the sidewalk policemen with diplomatic nightsticks held back the peasantry, gathered to gape at the great. Over their heads the blue smoke began to billow out under the marquee and spill upwards through the crimson glare of neon light letters that spelled out:

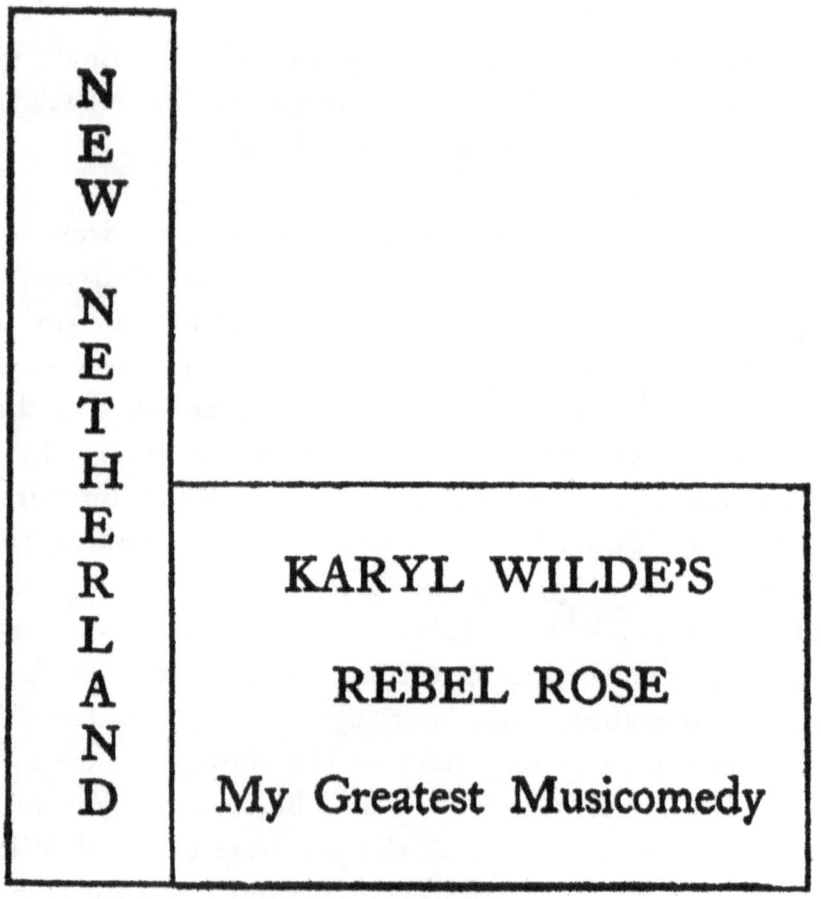

NEW NETHERLAND

KARYL WILDE'S

REBEL ROSE

My Greatest Musicomedy

"Curtain going up!"

A thousand cigarettes puffed faster, the roar of voices rose higher, as the shivering scores in the vestibule funneled through to jam into the hundreds milling in the lobby.

Two men found a haven behind the brass rail in front of the closed box office. One was huge and ruddy, a bulldog in tweeds and soft-collared blue shirt, with a jolly, jowled face and weary blue eyes. A dramatic critic, he appeared, rather, to be an English country squire. The other was a head shorter, lean, with wiry, greying hair and shaggy eyebrows over twinkling dark eyes like a Scottish terrier's; he wore dress clothes of a conservative cut. He looked to be a schoolmaster; he was the eastern public relations counsel for Ponderous Pictures, no less.

"A brilliant assemblage," said the big man, tartly. "So many men in tails would be a great comfort to Darwin."

The Scottie gave this a flicker of a smile.

"Not to speak of apes and gorillas." He lowered his voice. "Did you hear that pair talking about Twitchell, behind me?"

"No. What?"

"One of them said: 'Did you read his column today? He's on his way out and don't know it.' And the other one said: 'He don't look like a bad little guy, at that.' And the other one said: 'You can put that on a wreath, if you want to. It's silver handles for him. I'm tellin' you.'"

"How do you know they meant Twitchell? Was that all they said?"

"I was fool enough to look around, and they shut up tight and moved off."

"Know who they were?"

"No. Just a couple of anthropoids."

"Probably two producers talking about Georgie Jean."

"Don't be funny, Perry. I'm going to talk to Ted Edwards about this."

"What can he do?"

"He can make Tommy listen to reason and take on a bodyguard."

"A muscle man, eh? I'd rather be shot than have one dog me around. You must be coming down with paranoia, Wylie. You've been seeing too many gangster movies."

Wylie shook his head, compressed his lips stubbornly.

"It's a hunch. I've always laughed 'em off before—these predictions that Tommy won't live a week or even a month. I've even collected bets on it. But I'm getting goose flesh, lately."

"You're tired, Wylie. Why don't you ever get a night's sleep?"

"I'm turning in early tonight, but I'm going to talk to Edwards first."

"Well, he was sitting about four rows behind us. And I saw him going downstairs towards the men's room as we came out."

"I'll catch him at home by phone. He's giving a party tonight, after the show. It's funny: I woke up last night thinking about Tommy. I started to pick up the phone and call Edwards, but it was four o'clock and I was afraid he'd be asleep."

"Well, of course," said Perry Hamilton. "Tommy's a valuable piece of property for a publisher. A lot of the *Blade's* circulation is due to him."

"Edwards figures at least fifty thousand papers a day, and double that on Mondays when he prints his hot gossip."

Hamilton whistled. "As much as that? What does he pay Twitchell? Or is that a fair question?"

"Tommy makes no secret of it. It's a thousand a week now."

"If you say so, it's true."

"I read the contract. He just signed a three-year renewal. He's syndicated, besides, to about seventy-five papers. With radio and magazine side money, he's taking close to a hundred grand a year."

"That's twice what you and I make, together, and we're overpaid, God knows. How does he rate it?"

"There's only one of him and the public eats his stuff. He's a superb gossip. Mainly, I think, because the human race never ceases to amaze and amuse him."

"He'll likely die of gout and good living at eighty."

"He can't," said King. "He'll wear out, he'll break down or go crazy if he keeps up this pace."

"If he lasts out the three years, he ought to be able to retire rich. Does he save his money?"

"Most of it. He could cash in tomorrow for two hundred grand, at least. He owns the penthouse he lives in; that's forty thousand or so."

"He ought to quit. I'm going to retire on less than that, in a few years."

"Exactly. That's what Tommy says. In a few years he'll quit. Like hell! You'll stay with it until you have to sit on the aisle in a wheel chair. And me! Twenty years of pictures, and I'm looking forward to television. Three Broadway dopes!"

"How does Tommy get all that intimate stuff he puts out on Mondays? I've asked him, but he just grins and says: 'I never reveal a source.' Shall we move in?" They joined the stragglers coming in from the vestibule.

"Tommy works like a bird dog," King replied, as they shuffled along. "He tries to see all and know all, like your Sunday school idea of God. But, of course, he can't. He gets a lot of his stuff from volunteer helpers, like me. We all like to show how much we know, and it gives us a secret satisfaction to see our indiscretions in print. Some people turn in scandal on themselves: little bounders who want to seem important, and ladies of the half-world whose vogue depends upon advertising. Then they yell like hell about it and buy a hundred copies of the paper. Women tell on each other, and men, too. That's the most dangerous— envy, jealousy and spite-work items."

"It seems to me it would keep Edwards poor paying off libel suits."

"You'd be surprised how seldom they get stuck. Tommy throws out ten times as much as he prints."

"Even at that—"

"The point is, Perry, that he writes mainly about people who are used to seeing their names in print, for better or worse. You analyze any of his Monday columns. They're about the high-hats, the bigwigs, the strutters and the posturers of the world that supports Broadway, and about the primitive types, the moronic and sub-normal people, the queer children who work in the Seven Arts, and particularly in the art of living without work. It's a mixture of sex, money, talent, asininity, perversion and crime, with a very little sincerity, this Broadway of ours. They call Times Square the double-crossroads of the world; have you ever reflected, Perry, that all the roads from the high places of the earth do cross here?"

"What amazes me," said the critic, "is that Twitchell, writing this intimate gossip in the most mixed, unstable and shifting place in the world, should create the interest he does."

"New York," said King, sententiously, "is a huge village with no town pump, no general store with cracker boxes, no sewing circle. People don't know their neighbors, so they can't hang over the back fence and gossip. But there's a human craving for gossip that has to be satisfied, somehow. That's what made Tommy's column catch on so fast. And now it burns its own smoke. All kinds of people slip him tips, and gags. He told me once how a bishop tried to get him to print the dirt on another bishop—professional jealousy."

"Didn't he print it?"

"He won't monkey with religious stuff—it's dynamite. And you may have noticed that he'll never tell on a married man unless the wife knows it and they're separated. He doesn't want to break up homes."

"Quixotic, in a way. People don't give him credit for it."

"He does have a strain of Don Quixote in him. You'll notice he delights in telling about the corporations, and the rich and the mighty grinding the faces of the poor. He'll break a lance any time on a good windmill. Sound journalism for mass circulation. Joe Pulitzer knew it; Hearst knows it; Edwards knows it."

"Is Edwards still losing money on the *Blade?*"

"He says not. For a corn belt publisher, he's done damn' well in the big town. He had the sense to hire Twitchell, for one thing."

They were passing through the innermost doors now, surrendering their intermission checks to a ticket-taker who kept up a chant of: "No smoking inside, please!" The black and white tiles at his feet were almost covered with cigarette butts, half of them stained with lipstick. Inside, they wormed their way along the wall to the door of the coatroom and planted themselves to wait until the crowd was seated. The crowd wasn't in any hurry about it, although the orchestra was trying to lure them down the aisles.

"Go on with what you were saying about Twitchell," Hamilton prompted. "That's good copy you're talking. You ought to write a piece on it for *Vanity Fair.*"

King grinned. "Old stuff to you, Perry."

"On the contrary; after ten years on Broadway, I'm still a hick. What you say about the prominent people not suing for libel is good sense, though. In my days as a reporter out in Chicago I found that out. The person to look out for is Mrs. Glizinski, of the stockyards set, who wants to shake you down for getting her mixed up with a madame of the same name in a three-line police court item. I suppose very few of Tommy's victims would look like injured innocence to a jury of plain citizens."

"Moreover," said King, "the defense might try to show that the plaintiff didn't have a very good name to blacken, and that'd be awkward. It would for me, I know. But, you won't find much actionable stuff in his columns. He talks about infatuations, marriages on whim and divorces on second thought, scoops on the stork, human oddities, vanities, exhibitionism of all sorts. He shoots mostly at targets that are open to the public, anyway. Decent, respectable folk don't make good copy; nobody knows who they are. The others call it publicity or fame, and grin and bear it."

"Well, then, who's likely to kill him, Wylie? You make him out a public benefactor."

"I'll venture to say there are twenty men and twenty women in this audience who'd be glad to see him rubbed out, though they wouldn't dare take their grievances into court. If he were killed right here tonight, I wouldn't know whom to suspect nor where to begin. But what a story it would make!"

"Just a Broadway boy!" Hamilton scoffed. "You've got a heart as big as the Paramount Building, but you'd call it a good story if one of your best friends got shot! You really had a lot to do with starting him, didn't you, Wylie? I hear he learned his Broadway letters at your knee?"

King demurred, shaking his head.

"Not so much. When Tommy came back from Europe five years ago, with his living to make for the first time in his life, he did come to me for advice and between us we invented this job of town crier for him. I helped him get started, yes, but his stuff caught on very fast. First it was read only on Broadway, then on Park Avenue, and then the self-styled sophisticates all over town took it up, and within a couple of years papers all over the States were buying it, just so the local bloods could feel that they knew all about the New York celebrities."

The critic smiled, sourly.

"What a shock it must be to see your idols in the flesh when you come in from the country. It was to me, I know. Celebrities are such common looking dopes."

"Well, a lot of tourists are with us tonight. That fellow over there with the big smoked pearls in his shirt; he's a steel man from Pittsburgh. That mild little fellow who looks like an undertaker from Indianapolis—the one with the dowdy wife in blue—he's the head of a drug syndicate that imports a ton a year; he lives in Detroit. That pale lad over there who looks like a priest having a night out is the personal rod-carrier for the Crown Prince of Chicago. Hello, there's Tommy!"

Mr. Twitchell was standing twenty feet from them, near the head of a stairway up which the press of people was still pouring into the promenade, and against the short wall that separated it from the north stairway to the balcony, up which another stream was flowing.

A lone mongoose in a nest of cobras, he appeared, nevertheless, to be utterly at his ease, until you noticed his watchful, darting eyes. He was of average height and without distinction except for his silvered hair. His face, pale with the mazda tan of night life, was young and keenly alive, as was his whole dapper figure. His hands were thrust into his dinner jacket pockets, nonchalantly.

"Curtain going up! Please take your seats!"

The stragglers were beginning to thin out; contraband cigarettes were being crushed into the carpet. Ushers were herding the standees into the squares fenced off with plush ropes. The buzz of two thousand voices, from the front row up to the top balcony, almost drowned out the orchestra.

Twitchell, spying King and Hamilton through a gap in the passing stream, waved a salute. The two returned it, smiling.

King nudged Hamilton. "Pipe the dicks, trying to look like gentlemen. There must be a million in snatchable

stones on these dames. Here comes the current scandal. I
see he's wearing his wife in public these days. America has
always stood for the sanctity of the home. We insist upon
private hypocrisy in our public men."

Hamilton snorted.

"You know too much to be happy, Wylie. Look at me: a
serene suburbanite, too dumb to be indignant. All I know
is what I see in the tabloids, and sometimes I'm not even
sure of that."

"Well, you know who that girl in black is, don't you?"

Hamilton nodded. "Cheeky of her to show herself here
tonight," he said, wryly.

His eyes lingered on her voluptuous camellia-white
flesh, poured into the sheath of a black gown. The Blessed
Damozel had leaned on the bar too long before she came
to the theatre. A sleek eunuch of the London stage was
saying something simple into her unheeding ear; she was
staring with drunken intensity at the nodding, beaming
wife of the man whose mistress she was. She spied Twitchell; the two men heard her curse as she swept on.

Behind her sailed in a golden galleon from overseas,
back from a pirate raid on the treasures of Hollywood,
with a fat tug of a motion picture tycoon puffing along
beside her and, in her wake, the hot-eyed Levantine who
was her director, lover, and worst friend.

"My honored employer and his new star," Wylie mur-
mured, and bowed, smiling. The lady beamed upon the
nice Meester Keeng; her watch dog glared at him.

"He's jealous even of press agents who put their profane hands on pictures of her," King muttered, grinning.

Here came a madonna out of a Botticelli painting who
wrote, with a lancet dipped in the perfumed venom of her
own pet cobras, little masterpieces to prove that a wise
woman should never share her bed with a man; she was
staring snootily at a hoyden from the films who, everyone

knew, seldom slept alone, because she was afraid of the
dark, and men were such fun anyway. After her shuffled
an emaciated figure who looked like an evangelist, but
who Wylie knew was a heroin addict and a killer. Jack
Jordan's Man Friday. King felt his spine tingling, but the
grim reaper passed without looking at him. Here came a
more pleasant sight: a blond, sunburned boy whose goal
in life was to make the international polo team, and at the
same time, every girl in the Wilde chorus. Wylie winked
at him; the lad saluted with drunken gravity. Here came
the son of a really great man, whose only ambition, Wylie
knew, was to seduce the olive-skinned dancer who was
clinging to his arm. The girl, Twitchell had told him, was
a high-brown from Harlem, passing as Spanish on Broadway. Tommy had been debating, as Wylie knew, whether
he ought to expose her, and had decided that it was none
of his business, even if the boy married her. She knew that
Tommy knew all about her, yet she apparently had smiled
at him, for Tommy bowed to her urbanely.

Here loomed up Emanuel (Big Manny) Murillo, Roman
of face, Greek of body, London-perfect in dress: a visiting
power from Chicago, incognito; his wife was the baby-
faced tap-dancer in tonight's leg opera. He strode over
to Tommy with the pantherine grace of a Dempsey, and
said something to him. Tommy nodded. Murillo moved
on. Tommy had taken his hands out of his pockets and was
standing as though poised to move, in perplexed thought.
King's eyes followed the Crown Prince's oiled black head
as he wove his way back toward the lobby door and disappeared through it. When Wylie turned back, Tommy had
vanished.

"Let's get down to our pews," Hamilton suggested.
"This crowd will never get settled until the act begins."

"It should have by now. I wonder if anything's gone
wrong backstage."

As they turned toward the head of the aisle they were confronted by another striking figure, this one crowned by a flamboyant mop of red hair. He had just emerged from the aisle, against traffic; the foppish fit of his tailcoat, waistcoat, and shirt was disarranged. He seized Wylie's arm.

"Have you seen Tommy?" he demanded, looking around as he inquired.

"Yes," said King. "He was standing over there, next to the stairs, just a minute ago."

"Which way did he go?"

"I didn't notice. Shane, do you know Perry Hamilton? This is Shane O'Neal, Perry."

They shook hands. "I haven't the honor," Shane boomed, "though I'm one of his great admirers. You'll excuse me, Mr. Hamilton; I've got to find a man right away." He smiled, bowed, turned, hurried off. The promenade was almost clear of stragglers now; the standees meekly confined within the plush ropes, like bunches of human asparagus.

"The grand manner!" said Hamilton, grinning. "Who is he? Not an actor?"

"Shane does act like an actor," said Wylie, as they turned into the head of the aisle. "He's the radio baritone. You must have heard him."

"No," said the critic. "But my wife's crazy about him. I never listen to the damned radio myself, but she even goes to his concerts at Carnegie Hall. Is he really so good?"

"He's made a reputation—and a small fortune—out of a fair voice, good looks, a professional Irish manner and a fine sense of showmanship," said King. He grinned. "That sounds catty. I'm very fond of Shane. He's a great friend of Tommy's; they own the two penthouses on top of the Park-Tower, you know."

"You live there, too, don't you?"

"Only halfway up the Tower. I'm not a penthouse type. Too rich for my blood."

They slid into the seats next to the aisle in the second row, right center. The house lights, dimming down to a yellow glow, faded out. Baby spotlights leaped down through the dark and revealed the usual two pianists at the usual two pianos in the pit who played, in *reprise,* "My Rebel Rose," the waltz song from the first act, patent-leather heads flashing in the spotlight. They ended to loud applause; rose, bowed, retired. The orchestra took up the introduction to the second act.

The footlights glowed up, and died away; the lofty drapes, suffused with violet light, slid apart to disclose a cyclorama of the harbor of Rio de Janeiro, the world's most beautiful water gate. Stars burned cold in the blue-black void, the lights of the city twinkled in a far-flung crescent around the bay; presently dawn began to gray the sky behind Sugar Loaf Mountain. The stars paled out. The Brazilian delegation from Washington, sitting in a flag-draped box, applauded diplomatically.

Hamilton focused a miniature flash light on his program; King leaned over and read: "The Rebel Camp on Corcovado Mountain, overlooking the capital of San Bolivario; dawn, a week later."

Far-off chanting and the mutter of distant drums. The rebels were marching on the capital. Swelling clearer and nearer the chant was punctuated now with the boom of distant cannon, the crackle of musketry. A tiny warship, up on the harbor cyclorama, began to flash fire and real smoke; amid the scream of shells and off-stage explosions, the toy rebel batteries on the distant heights fired back. The pungent smell of powder drifted out over an audience that was acting like children at a pantomime, shrieking, laughing, buzzing, holding hands over ears.

"Great showmanship," said King, drily. "Never saw better effects."

On came a rebel mob, pouring onto the stage, a rocky mesa overlooking the city, the chorus men as scarecrow soldiers, the dancers and show girls in revealing silken rags, anything but revolting. The baritone, immaculate in whites and scarlet sash, strode down stage, waving a sabre, and led in part-singing of the revolutionary marching song, to much stamping of feet and waving of *machetes*. Even though it sounded strangely like a medley from "The Vagabond King," "Song of the Flame," and "The Three Musketeers," with the Maine Stein Song, it was stirring.

Applause crashed, rolled, pattered, died out. The daughters of the revolution switched their silken tails into the background and a Ballet of Rebel Amazons ran onto the scene; cuddly little wild women, fresh from the jungle, clad in green parakeet's wings, four wings to a rebel. They fell back, in a tableau, and on floated the Queen of the Amazons, on her royal toes, in a costume representing, no doubt, the Triumph of Reason, since it was conspicuous by its absence. Something like a shiver of delight ran through the two thousand in the house. Here was a body among bodies, a grace to shame the Graces.

"Patricia," Hamilton leaned over to whisper to King, "must be a descendant of one of the Paris twins born in Troy while Helen was there."

"A very pretty thought. I'll tell her you said that."

"She can read it in the review in the morning," said Perry. "You don't think I'd pass up a pun as pretty as that. Is she a friend of yours?"

"I'm just an uncle. She's Tommy's girl, you know."

"No, I didn't. Look here, can't I be an uncle, too?"

"Don't leer, you old lecher, or I'll have to sock you. She's a sweet kid, and she's on the level."

Someone wrathfully shushed their murmuring, and they were silent until the dancers glided off, ran back, curtseyed, ran off. Patricia reappeared, sank to one knee, kissed her hand, vanished through the wings. Two thousand people felt a little cleaner, laved by youth and innocence.

The comedy relief! Pistol shots banging in the wings, right. Onstage plunged the terrified comedian, clutching the seat of his khaki shorts, at which two giants draped in cartridge belts were aiming bayoneted rifles. In Act One the funny man had been about to corner the Brazil nut market, make his million and win the acrobatic comedienne away from the dissolute old president of San Bolivario. Now he was under arrest as a capitalist, a friend of the old regime, an enemy of the people. The shopworn plot picked up its frayed ends and spun on.

"You can't shoot me!" piped the comedian, striking an attitude. "I'll tell Mr. Hoover and he'll sweep yer into the sea!"

The audience roared, relaxed. This was going to be good. The comedian tried another gag.

"Shoot, if you must this old grey head, but spare my Boy Scout pants, he said!"

Another roar. Wylie King leaned over to his host's ear.

"You don't mind if I go, do you, Perry? I want to catch the last scene across the street. I hear Starling sent 'em out on stretchers in Philadelphia."

"Go ahead. I wish I had gone over there tonight. One act of this is plenty. But Wilde would have sent the old man a three-page telegram whining about my neglect of his masterpiece, and the old man wouldn't be asked to Wilde's next Sunday School picnic."

"You're not so innocent! Call me up when you feel like chinning again. I've got a new speakeasy, where they know how to make *crepes suzettes*. And thank you kindly."

"Pleasure's mine, Wylie. Meeting of the best minds."

King sidled out past Perry's fat knees and catfooted up the aisle. He got his hat, coat and snakewood stick from the red-haired Hebe in the coatroom. As he passed the head of the basement lounge stairs he collided with the house fireman, who was keeping his eyes on the stage as he walked.

"Sorry," said the press agent, perfunctorily. "Excuse *me!*" the fireman said. He dodged around Mr. King and ran down the stairs.

King clicked out through the cold lobby, still stinking of stale smoke and a potpourri of perfumes. A porter was pushing a brush methodically across the cigarette-strewn tiles; a policeman stood on post before the box-office door and two more were pacing up and down inside the plate-glass doors of the vestibule.

King stopped at the curb to rub the muzzle of a policeman's horse; the officer standing by him saluted pleasantly.

"A cold night for you two," said Wylie.

"It is that, Mr. King. But we go off duty as soon as this show lets out, and the one acrost the way. They're both late."

"This one won't be out for another forty minutes. All Mr. Wilde's openings run an hour too long, Denny."

He looked at his watch; it was 11:41.

"And why would that be?" asked the policeman.

"He wants to see what Broadway likes in it before he throws away any part of the show. By the third night he'll cut an hour out of what he showed tonight."

"Well, if he's got any of them girls to throw away, I'll be waiting around by the ashcan."

Wylie chuckled. "Good night!" he said and stepped into the street, almost into the path of a speeding black limousine. He stepped back. As the car, brakes screaming, slid past him, he saw in it the lean, hawk-nosed, swarthy, birth-marked face of Jack Jordan, born Giovanni Giordani, one-time petty racketeer in Hell's Kitchen, now owner of the Del Oro Club and supposed head of the sacramental wine industry south of 125th Street in Manhattan. The Grape King, they called him. He was bare-headed and in dinner coat, without a topcoat.

The man in the cap, driving the car, Wylie did not recognize, though he turned his face to look back and curse at King. The car went on and turned down Seventh Avenue, to the right, against the traffic light.

Wylie waited his chance to cross the street between the on-rushing taxicabs. Not many pedestrians were out; the theatre crowds had vanished; the wind was too bitter. He walked into the lobby of the Nichols Theatre, where, according to the signs, Susan Starling was opening in a Daring Drama, *Burn the Woman*.

At 11:39 p.m., Nels Lundberg, the house fireman on duty at the New Netherland, ran down the broad marble staircase at the rear of the orchestra floor to the basement, after colliding in the promenade with the little gentleman who was leaving. It was a chore he should have performed immediately after intermission, to extinguish any live cigarette snipes carelessly thrown around in the lounge or washrooms. Nels had come down from the gallery and balcony inspection right after the rise of the curtain, but had lingered in the side aisle for some ten minutes, gripped by the beauty of the setting, and, no doubt, of the girls. Twenty-five, blond, burly and handsome, Nels was male and this was his first first night.

Downstairs, Nels went into the men's washroom through the slatted swinging door near the far end of the right hand wall of the hall. Paper towels, overflowing a huge iron trashcan, littered the floor around the wash basins. The fireman kicked around the litter until he was satisfied that there was no smoldering cigarette in it. As he pushed the door out someone tried to come through it from the hall. The man outside gave way.

It was the negro porter, carrying his brush broom.

"Where you been, boy?" the fireman asked, accusingly.

"Me and the maid we taken a little look upstairs. Ain't that swell scenery Mr. Wilde got for the openin' numbah?"

"Sure is," said the fireman, and strode on into the smoking lounge, done in the Oriental grand manner of the 'nineties. From tall Chinese jars, filled with white sand, a few lingering cigarettes were sending up thin plumes of blue smoke. Though there were several butts ground into the fine Chinese rug, none of them was smoldering.

The fireman paused at the door marked Ladies, rapped on it, waited, thrust in his head and shoulders. The maid was evidently still upstairs looking at the show. Coming out through the archway into the hall, he encountered the plump Negress. She grinned at him, guiltily. The fireman started upstairs. He happened to glance down over the banister.

Across one of the foot-square white tiles of the black-and-white checkerboard of the floor there showed a trickle of some dark liquid. As the fireman, halting, looked down at it, the end of it crawled crookedly across another white square. The fireman walked back down the steps and around the newel post.

Under the stairs were three standard telephone booths. In the middle one, a man was sitting, his crisp, brillian-tined silver hair shining in reflected light. The booth was dark, for the door, hinged in the middle to fold back, was not closed enough to make contact for the light inside. The man's face was turned partly away from the pane of glass through which the fireman was looking at him. Apparently he was waiting for a call to go through, for he was leaning forward, relaxed, with the side of his head against the coin telephone on the booth wall at the right. The fireman could see only his black coat, a strip of white collar, and the back of his head.

Apparently the gentleman had sat down too hard on his pocket flask. The fireman, grinning, bent over to test the liquor that had trickled out of the booth. It didn't smell of alcohol. He looked at it on his fingers. Thick, sticky. He smelled it again.

"Porter!" he called out.

The broom ceased thumping against the trash can. The porter emerged.

"There's a fellow in there hurt. That's blood on the floor!"

The porter shuffled across and peered through the pane, muttering. He rapped on the glass.

The man in the booth did not stir.

"Drunk, maybe, and cut hisself," hazarded the porter, trying vainly to open the booth door. The fireman took the handle in his big right hand, reached his left arm inside, moved the man's legs; the door flew back. The figure seated on the little bench in the left rear corner of the booth came toppling toward them.

Nels caught him, bent over to look into the face. The eyes were open, glassy; the head had fallen forward, the lower jaw sagging.

The fireman, his hands trembling, tipped up the chin. A powder burn covered the throat, spreading onto the wings of the collar. Under the chin, in the angle formed by the lower jaw bones, was a small hole. The fireman rested the body against his left arm and rolled the head around. The bullet had emerged about two inches above and behind the left ear, rather cleanly. There wasn't a great deal of blood in the thick, curly silver hair back there. The fireman put his ear to the shirt front, groped for a wrist, felt for a pulse.

The porter had retreated, mouth open. The fireman boosted the body back into the booth, restored it as nearly as possible to the position in which he had found it, stepped back, went up to turn the head a trifle more to the left where it rested against the telephone, closed the door, addressed the porter.

"Go get the house manager. Don't run. Take it easy. Keep your mouth shut. We don't want to start a panic."

The porter went up the stairs on tiptoe, looking back fearfully at the fireman, standing over the little rivulet of blood, arms folded across his dress coat. The end of the trickle had gone no farther across the tiles.

Footsteps on the stairs. A short, hard-faced fellow in dinner clothes was coming down much too fast for a man of his age. Nels recognized the house manager, with whom he had conferred when he came on duty.

"What's this? Somebody shot?" His face was almost purple.

"Dead! In the booth." Nels led him around to it.

The manager peered through the glass.

"How do you know he's dead? Get him out."

"We had him out. I put him back the way he was."

"Who shot him?"

"I don't know. I just happened to see the blood on the floor."

The manager wrenched at the booth door; it jammed again, halfway open. Nels caught his arm.

"I tell you he's dead, Mr. Flaxon. The thing to do is to leave him like he is until the police come."

Flaxon stepped back, uncertainly.

"Open the door, anyway," he said slowly. "Maybe I know him."

Nels managed to get the door open without disarranging the body.

Fig. I

(From The New York *Evening Blade*, Tuesday, January 26)

Scene of Twitchell Murder

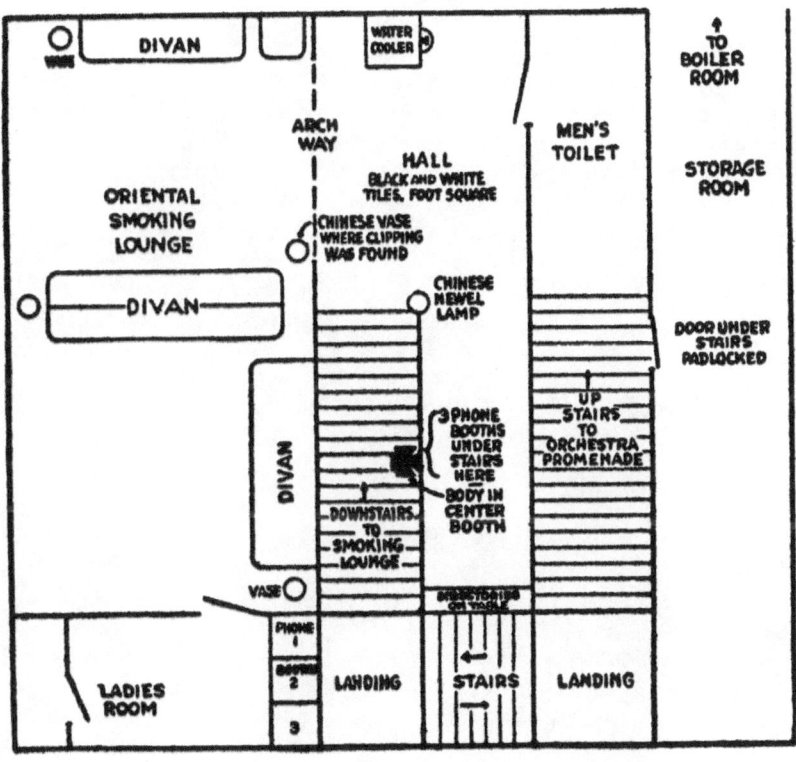

"Pull his face around, will you?" Flaxon snapped. Nels pulled out the torso against his left shoulder. Flaxon peered at the face.

"Good God! It's Tommy Twitchell!"

"The fellow that writes for the *Blade?*"

"Oh, my God, yes! And in my theatre!"

2

While Nels Lundberg had been going downstairs to find the body of Thomas Cary Twitchell, bachelor of this parish, town crier of Broadway, court jester of Bagdad-on-the-Make, in the telephone booth at the New Netherland Theatre, Wylie King had been stalking out through the lobby, lined with huge camera studies, by America's foremost photographer of female flesh, of Wilde beauties, past and present, as the retouching artist conceived their perfections. Now, at 11:43, he was in the lobby of the Nichols Theatre, across the street.

"Where's Mr. Gratz?" he asked the doorman.

"Still counting up." He started toward the box office, but the door opened and Gratz came out.

"Oh, hello, Wylie!" The company manager came over to shake hands.

"Anything left, inside?"

"Not a thing, unless some commuter's made a break for an early train. I'll ask the head usher. Were you across the street?"

King nodded. "I got enough of it."

"I heard it was a sure hit," said Gratz, surprised.

"You heard right. How's yours?"

"I think we're over for a run; maybe a hit. We opened against Wilde because Leo was leery of the first string

critics, but I wisht now we had 'em; I think they'd go for
it. It's old-fashioned hokey melodrama about the wronged
woman, but it's layin' 'em in the aisles. Of course, Starling's got a public that'd think she was great in *East Lynne*,
but this crowd is from the brokers and the hotels. I suppose you seen how we took the highbrows in Philly?"

"I read it in *Variety,*" said King. "Well, I hope Ponderous gets this. We need a good tear-jerker. The public's
swinging back to sentiment this year."

"Come on in, and I'll see if I can park you."

There was, it developed, only one seat vacant, on the
right aisle just behind a box, and set off from the rest of
the row by a balcony pillar. Someone hadn't stayed for the
third act. Wylie took off his overcoat, put on his spectacles, settled down. The last act was approaching its climax;
the audience was taut as a fiddle string. Smart people, too,
to judge by the women's clothes.

Ten minutes later Wylie found himself, rather to his
surprise, standing up and pounding his palms. There were
cheers as Sue Starling, her makeup streaked with real tears,
came out to bow, again and again, brought out the leading
man, the troupe of six one by one, then came out herself
for three bows, then dragged on the author and chubby
Leo Turnbow, the producer.

Wylie turned to move out ahead of the crowd. There
was something white under his feet: a handkerchief. He
stooped and picked it up. His shoes had begrimed it, but
such fine lace bordered the little square of cambric that
he didn't toss it down. Good taste in perfume, too. He'd
have it cleaned and give it to Patsy Paris. He stuck it into
his pocket, got into the aisle, shrugged into his overcoat
and hurried out while the author was making a fumbling
speech of thanks.

He passed Herman Gratz in the lobby. "You've got a
hit—I don't have to see the first of it to tell you that," he

called across. Herman grinned, shook his own hand over his head like a prizefighter. Wylie saluted with his silver-headed snakewood stick and went out into the bitter west wind. The Wilde show across the way wasn't out yet. He turned west to Times Square, the wind blowing him along, gave up when he had crossed the Square, hailed a taxi.

"Park Tower," he said, and slumped back in his seat. He was weary of wine, women and what have you. Tonight he would spend in peace, in his own cooperatively owned castle, with the last volume of Marcel Proust, which he'd been reading at for a month. He'd be at home by a quarter after twelve, for the first time in weeks.

The fireman pushed back into the middle booth under the stairway the body of Tommy Twitchell. He arranged the arms and legs and head as they had been, closed the folding door, leaving it an inch ajar, stepped back and viewed his work with satisfaction.

He was thinking: If I can do some smart work here, maybe I can get a transfer to the police and be a detective.

"This is a big murder," Nels said, his voice trembling a little. "It'll make a big story in the papers."

"My God, yes!" the house manager exploded, the blood rushing back into his white face. "It'll be on every front page in the world tomorrow. But what'll it do to the show? It can't help us; we got a sixteen weeks buy now, but they might stay away."

"They won't stay away," said Nels, grimly. "They can't get in to see where the body was found without buying a ticket, can they? You'll have to call out the reserves to keep 'em out. I don't know anything about your business, but I know this town. You take a fire where there's been some people burned up—"

"I guess you're right," Frank Flaxon cut in. "I've been in show business thirty-two years and manager of this house twelve, but I never had a man shot on me before. And a man like Twitchell! On opening night! My God, Karyl'll go nuts! He's nuts anyway, on an opening night. And no matinee until Thursday. We ought to have an extra one Wednesday. Tomorrow we got to rehearse and cut the show—" He was thinking aloud.

"Look here," Nels interrupted. "We got to call the police."

Laughter came rolling down the stair well from the auditorium, like summer thunder.

Flaxon looked at the fireman, swallowed, licked his dry lips. "They mustn't know about this. We got to wait until the show breaks," he said, weakly.

"I wouldn't try that, Mr. Flaxon," said Nels. "You'd get in wrong. The police ought'a been called before this."

From his dinner-coat pocket, Flaxon brought out a silk handkerchief. He took off his black felt hat and wiped the streaming sweat from his forehead, under the thin hair, dyed blue black.

"I'll get Wilde," he said, dully. "It's up to him. It's his show. You stay here. Throw some paper towels over that blood on the floor. If anybody comes down, you stand in front of that booth."

He shuffled around to the stairs and plodded unsteadily up, clutching the banister rail.

Hurrying into the washroom, Nels grabbed a handful of paper towels from a dispensing box, came out and crossed the hall. He stood looking down at the rivulet drying on the alternate big black and white linoleum tiles of the checkerboard floor. In the detective stories he read constantly at the firehouse, a great point was made of touching nothing near the body until the police came. He couldn't see, however, that the trickle of blood would furnish any clue. He got down on his knees so he could study the course of it across the one black square and the two white squares it traversed.

Nobody had stepped in it. But, of course, the murderer would have escaped long before any blood had overflowed from the floor of the telephone booth. He laid the absorbent paper over the coagulated blood. Some showed through. He went back to the washroom, got more towels and covered the stained ones.

Footsteps on the stairs. A young gentleman in a tail coat, rather uncertain where his feet were leading him, plunged across the hall to the men's room. Presently he came out, stopped at the water cooler. The cup machine clicked several times, was punched viciously.

"Whyn't they put 'nuf cupsinthesethings?" he demanded of the fireman, who was keeping his broad torso between this youth's uncertain vision and the telephone booth.

"Try puttin' in a penny."

"T'besure," said the youth, swaying. "You got a penny? Never take a penny, myself. Keep the change, I always say. Keep the change!"

Nels maneuvered across, put a penny in the cup machine, filled the cup at the tap. The gilded youth drained and refilled it, spilled water on his shirt, gulped.

"'Swonderful," he confided. "Wha's your name, fireman?"

"Why?" Nels grinned, by force.

"Send you back the penny, stupid! You smoke cigars?"

"Sure do." Anything to get rid of this menace.

"Send my chauf'r over tomorrow with fine box cigars and penny in th' top, like John D. Rockf'ler's book. You ever read a book, fireman?"

"Sure. Detective stories. Murder—" He stopped abruptly.

"Goin' mur'r a fellow myself soon's I catch up on my drinkin'. Been in hosp't'l. Got way behind on drinkin'."

"You better be gettin' back upstairs. You'll miss half the act."

"Wha'f I do? Gotta see this dam' show thousand times. Gotta fr'en' in the chorus. Mary's li'l lamb. . . . Everywhere that Mary went the lamb was sure to go." He laughed, hilariously. Nels had to laugh with him; it was contagious.

"Not much time left for your work," he said.

"Don' have to work. Old man's lousy with sugar. In th' sugar business. Mos'ly in Havana. Wonderful city, Havana. Ever been in Havana, fireman? Was' your name? You di'n tell me your name?"

"Nels Lundberg, Engine Company No. 21."

"Wha' you do when you're workin'?"

"Pipeman. On the hose."

"Squirt the hose? If I was you I'd get a job steerin' hook-'n-ladder. Won'erful job, steerin' hook-la'r. Zip! Go roun' corner! Zip! 'Nother corner." He lurched and skidded across the tiles, illustrating the technique of steering the hook-and-ladder. This brought him to the foot of the stairs, fortunately.

"Where's th' elevat'r?" he demanded.

"No elevator. Walk up! One foot at a time. Up you go!" Nels gave him a boost.

"'S lousy!" complained the sugar boy, setting his feet carefully and clinging to the rail with both hands. "You pay hun'r'd dollars for seat in firs' row, and the lousy thea'r makes you walk up stairs. Tha's Bro'way. Jus' a lotta gyps."

At the first landing he turned and pointed dramatically down to Nels.

"If your name's Lin'berg, what you doin' in the fire 'partment?"

Nels shrugged and grinned. If he could only throw this guy out the front door! But the guy was on his way. Nels went back to his post.

Silence. Another roar of laughter rolling downstairs.

Clicking heels on the stairs. A woman coming down. Nels stayed where he was, planted in front of that booth, though he couldn't see her from where he stood. Better not risk alarming a woman. He could hear her voice, echoing around through the archway, and the negro maid's voice, too. The maid was supplying her with change. Nels heard a telephone booth door grate shut on the women's side of the lounge. Silence again.

Another man was coming down. He sighted the fireman as he stopped to draw a cup of water.

"Swell show, eh?" he said, amiably. "But I reckon you see a lot of shows."

"Sorry," said Nels, from in front of the tragic booth. "Can't talk on duty."

"That's New York for you!" snapped the portly citizen, and waddled into the washroom, muttering.

Two men were hurrying down the stairs. Nels couldn't see them; he was still blocking the line of vision from the washroom door to that telephone booth. Around the tall newel post, topped with its elaborate Chinese lantern that cast a pattern of colored lights on the tiles, came Flaxon, with a tall, stooped, broad-shouldered, grizzled man of perhaps fifty, beginning to go fat around the middle. He was in a grey lounge suit with a light green, soft-collared shirt and a pale green, four-in-hand tie, brown shoes and dark green velour hat. Nels had seen him backstage, wandering around like an unhappy ghost before the performance, giving orders in a weary snarl.

"This is Mr. Wilde," said Flaxon, unnecessarily. "This fireman found him. Clarence came and got me."

Nels gathered that Clarence was the colored porter. He stepped aside from the booth. The producer shot a glance through the glass in the door and turned his back on it.

"I don't want to look at him," he said shuddering visibly. "I'm a wreck, already," he complained in a nasal whine, "and now this has to happen! You haven't called the police, Frank? I don't want my audience disturbed."

"We've got to call the police, Karyl. This is murder."

"Well, tell 'em to come in quietly, for God's sake. Wait a minute! I sent a pair to the Commissioner—a pair of my own seats. Did he come?"

"I didn't see him," Flaxon said, "but I can find out quick." He started upstairs.

"Don't let anybody hear you. Just tell him I want him down here."

Nels whirled around. The portly gentleman had emerged from the washroom. His face brightened. Advancing, he spoke:

"Mr. Wilde, you don't know me, but I've been coming to your shows for twenty years. I'm from Michigan—Saginaw, Michigan. I want to tell you that I think you've outdone yourself."

Wilde had advanced on the portly gentleman, seized his elbow, turned the full candlepower of his smile on the upturned moon face and was propelling him up the stairs before the man got out the first ten words.

"You're very kind, very kind!" Halting on the first landing, Wilde shook his hand. "Will you excuse me? I'm having a little argument with the fireman about so many standees. Not even the police reserves can keep the American public out of my shows. Will you give my regards to anyone in Saginaw who remembers me—and come again."

"I certainly will, Mr. Wilde. I certainly will!" The cheery voice trailed off and up.

The producer walked heavily down the flight and dropped onto the broad lower step.

"My God!" he exploded. "Is there anybody else down here?"

"Woman on the ladies' side, telephoning," said Nels. "And the maid."

"Go up and stand at the head of the staircase. Tell people that want to come down to go up to the balcony lounge. Tell 'em the plumbing's out of order. Tell 'em a water pipe busted. No, you send a boy for the head usher and he'll attend to it. You better come back down. If that woman in there tries to talk to me, there'll be another murder. Are you sure the fellow's not hiding down here?"

Nels stopped on the second step.

"Where could he hide?"

"Did you look in the washroom?"

Nels explored the washroom, came back, shaking his head.

"That door," said Wilde, pointing to an iron one in the wall opposite the telephone booths. "It's always kept locked. Try it, anyway."

It was locked.

"It's padlocked on the other side," Wilde said. "It leads out through the engine room. There's no way out on the ladies' side. We better not disturb those women. I'd rather have a mad dog in a theatre than a screaming woman."

There were voices and footsteps on the stairs.

"Go on up and tell the head usher," Wilde reminded Nels.

On the landing the fireman encountered Flaxon and a burly six-footer in a tuxedo with a shirt front as big as Times Square. Not the police commissioner, but a big shot evidently.

Flaxon caught at the fireman's sleeve.

"This man found the body," he said. "Where you going, fireman?"

"To tell the head usher to keep people from coming down. Mr. Wilde's orders."

"I attended to that," said Flaxon, petulantly. "Come on with us. This is Inspector Maguire, in charge of the Homicide Squad."

Wilde got up from the bottom step.

"There's hell to pay here, Barney," he whined. "Did Frank tell you?"

The inspector nodded. "Where is he?"

"I put him back in the booth just like we found him, as soon as we were sure he was dead," Nels volunteered.

The inspector shot a keen glance at him under the bushy eyebrows, grotesquely black in the expanse of his huge face and bald forehead.

"Who's we?" They were moving around to the booths now.

"The colored porter. I called him."

"Where's he now?"

"I don't know," said Flaxon. "Shall I get him?"

"Never mind, yet. Anybody else down here when you found him?"

The inspector opened the booth, scrutinized the body as he talked. He avoided using the door handle; Nels had put his bare fingers on it, he remembered, guiltily.

"The maid was in the ladies' room. She and the porter had just come downstairs when I saw the blood on the floor."

"What blood?" The inspector looked around.

Nels indicated the litter of towels in front of the booth.

"We covered it up so nobody would see it."

"I took that liberty, Inspector," Flaxon put in, nervously. "I didn't want anybody screeching down here and starting a panic upstairs."

"Can't be helped now," said the inspector. He stooped to peer under the chin, put a handkerchief over his fingers, turned the head carefully, checked the place where the bullet had gone out.

"I looked at the blood, Inspector, before I covered it up," Nels volunteered. "Nobody had stepped in it. I got down on my hands and knees and looked."

"I thought you were a fireman," said the inspector, shooting him a shrewd glance. "We've got to leave the body as it is for the medical examiner. You sure you got it back just as it was?"

"Yes, sir. I knew that was important."

"There's been so many of these lousy detective books lately," the Inspector growled to Wilde, "that even a fireman thinks he's a Sherlock Holmes."

That crack didn't seem necessary. Nels gave up the idea of helping on this case and working for a transfer to the police. This Maguire was just a bull, full of himself.

"You're sure there wasn't anybody else down here when you found the body?" Nels was being quizzed again.

"I didn't think to look," he replied, slowly. "But if anybody was here, he's still here. I've been down here every minute since then, and the stairs are the only way in or out."

"Anybody come down since you found him?"

"Two gentlemen. One was in full dress. He was drunk. One woman went in the ladies' side. I heard her come down; I didn't see her. She's still in there."

"We'll see her as she comes out. Could you identify either of the men?"

"One was a sap from Saginaw, Michigan," Wilde cut in. "He wouldn't kill a fly. He talked to me about the show. I'll spot him for you, as they go out, if you want him. But you'd be wasting your time."

The inspector returned to Nels.

"The drunk one—what did he look like?"

"He was a blond young fellow. I didn't notice much. Looked like a collar ad."

"With very English, baggy pants and an extra-long tail coat, like an actor?" Flaxon spoke up. "And a gardenia in his lapel?"

"What's a gardenia?" Nels asked.

"Didn't you ever see Grover Whalen?" the inspector demanded, severely.

"That's right," said Nels. "He talked to me; I like to never got rid of him. Said his father's in the sugar business."

"Exactly," said Flaxon. "I'll vouch for him. We had to take him backstage to keep him quiet during the first act. That's Happy Carewe." He turned to Maguire.

"Just a polo player, Inspector. Perfectly harmless, drunk or sober."

"How did you know he was drunk?" the Inspector shot at Nels.

"I don't. He had a whiskey breath and he walked and talked drunk, that's all."

"Never be sure of anything, son. Now, it stands to reason that whoever shot Twitchell did it after the second act curtain went up and the crowd was all out of here. What's your name?"

"Nels Lundberg. Pipeman, Engine Company No. 21."

"Good outfit. Your Captain's a friend of mine."

Nels swallowed.

"Well, maybe you won't tell him I stayed upstairs so long after the curtain went up before I made my rounds down here. He'd raise hell. I just couldn't keep from looking at the show."

Wilde smiled wanly. Praise was praise.

"I think we can fix that," said the inspector. "Do you know just what time you came down here?"

"I started down at 11:39. I looked at my watch."

"When did your second act start, Karyl?"

"At exactly 11:30. I was backstage raising hell about it. There was a dancer wasn't ready. She had to go on right after the opening. She—"

The producer stopped talking. An odd look passed across his face.

"She what?" Maguire prompted him.

"That's all. I had to fine the girl. First time she was ever late for anything."

"So that's why we went up so late," said Flaxon. "Who was the girl?"

"I'll tell you later. We're holding up the Inspector."

The inspector was fumbling in his trouser pockets. He brought out a palmful of coins.

"I never know where I put my money in these cast-iron overalls," he growled. "Any of you got a nickel? I'll have to get the homicide squad up here, now, Karyl. If Frank'll tell your doorman to let 'em in quietly and send 'em down to me and keep his mouth shut, the audience needn't know they're here."

Nels had three nickels. The inspector took them absently and went on talking:

"There'll be Dr. Martinez and a man with a camera. And Flaxon—go out and get the first cop you see and send him down to me. Not a traffic officer, you understand, nor a mounted man. Any Mick with a nightstick."

"Yes, sir," said the house manager. "There's some in the lobby, to watch the box office. But I'll get a man off the street, if I can find one."

"Pick up the porter and send him down, if he's not in Harlem by now," the inspector called after Flaxon.

"I've got to go backstage," said Wilde, irritably. "You don't need me, do you, Barney?"

"Go ahead. Meet me inside the front doors just before the show breaks up. I won't need you until then. Send down somebody to bring me up, if I'm not there. I want to look over some of these babies upstairs. You sure are gettin' high class trade these days, Karyl. I spotted twenty rats on the first floor we ought to have fried years ago. If we frisked the whole audience for rods, I'd guarantee you two dozen."

"You don't mean to do that?" Wilde demanded, alarmed.

"No, I don't mean to do that. What's the use? They've all got permits to shoot cops." He snorted.

There were advantages, Nels reflected, in being a fireman. Nobody ever shot a fireman, except some woman's husband, maybe.

Wilde followed Flaxon upstairs.

"I ought to make my rounds, again, Inspector," Nels suggested.

"All right, son. Don't leave the theatre, and don't talk to anybody."

Nels ran upstairs as the inspector went into the telephone booth next the rear wall.

The woman who had been telephoning in the ladies' room presently walked up the stairs while that exit was unwatched for the first time since the discovery of the body. The ushers at the head of the stairs had orders to stop persons going down, not any coming up. She vanished into the perfect concealment offered an undistinguished woman among thousands of her general appearance in the city of New York.

Coming back after ten minutes, finding the inspector still telephoning in the booth, Nels thought he would have a look around the lounge. The maid had evidently gone upstairs. He went into the ladies' room, and examined the transom that opened up into the court. Half of it was covered with sheet iron, around an electric ventilating fan; the other half with an inch-mesh screen of steel wire a quarter of an inch thick. No chance of getting through that without tools and plenty of work. There was an iron grating atop the ventilating shaft in the court pavement; Nels could see a heavy padlock and chain securing it. Nothing in the ladies' room.

Going back into the lounge, he cast around like a bird dog. Near the telephone booths, on the Chinese rug, he found a woman's handkerchief. Initialed *N;* no perfume. A plain hemstitched square of linen. He put it in his pocket.

As he shuffled through the archway, eyes on the floor, Nels spied, at the foot of the tall Chinese vase at the corner, a ball of paper. He picked it up to throw it into the sand-filled jar, a receptacle for cigarette butts and burnt matches. Something made him want to examine it first. He unfolded the tight ball, sat down on the bottom step of the staircase, just around the archway post at the right, and spread the paper out on his knee.

It was the lower part of a newspaper page, torn jaggedly across the center. The side uppermost was devoted to a radio chatter column, local broadcast programs in fine print and advertisements of receiving sets and musical instruments. Nels turned it over.

The reverse side, except for some theatrical ads and the nude legs of several undressed beauties of the stage, was taken up by the lower two-thirds of Mr. Tommy Twitchell's Monday column of Broadway gossip, in which were related sundry facts about the great and the near-great. It was, Nels recognized, from that afternoon's *Blade*.

Nels had read the column at the firehouse, after he had come on duty at 6 o'clock that evening, on his night platoon shift. But he read the part on the fragment again. It was out of that afternoon's paper, all right.

"What you got there?" the inspector's bulk loomed over him.

Nels stood up.

"I picked it up off the floor around the corner there. I think maybe it's a clue."

The inspector took the torn page from him, studied it, studied Nels, half a smile playing around his mouth.

"I thought you said you were a fireman," he commented, drily. "Now maybe you'll find the gun he was shot with. I can't. Or did you, already?"

"No, sir," said Nels, gravely. "I know the gun ain't in— it is not in the telephone booth. I looked, before we put the body back."

An image came back to his memory.

"There was a piece of paper on the floor. I should 'a' picked it up," he volunteered.

"On the floor where?"

"On the floor in the booth." Nels was on his way around, the Inspector after him.

Carefully Nels opened the door, holding back the body with one hand. He dropped to his knees. The paper was partly under the left shoe of the dead man. He got his fingers wet and sticky, but he fished it out intact. It was the top third of Twitchell's column, of that date, headed:

Tommy Twitchell
You Don't Tell Me—

Like the other piece, it was creased in small squares where the page had been folded, but it was not crumpled as the other had been. Most of it was sticky and stained with blood. Nels handed the fragment to the inspector, who was holding the first discovery gingerly by one corner. Maguire brought the torn edges together. They fitted.

With both pieces held out before him, Inspector Maguire walked over to the table, along the end wall under the turn of the stairs, which held, chained to its top, all the volumes of the New York City telephone directory. He dropped the two fragments of newspaper onto one book, pushed them together with a pencil. He turned to scrutinize the fireman, who had followed him.

"I've always said," he informed Nels, darkly, "that all the brainy cops in New York must be in the fire department."

Nels blushed. This was the time to suggest that the fire department had one man, at least, who would like to be a detective. But the golden opportunity passed.

A large policeman came majestically down the stairs, night stick in hand, halted, saluted.

"Officer Brannigan, Inspector. You sent for me?"

"You're from West 47th Street?"

"Yes, sir. Was there a shooting down here?" He was looking around for any sign of a crime.

"If you must know, the corpse just went in the booth to call up his friends and say goodbye," the inspector informed him, glaring.

The patrolman preserved a straight face, with only a glance toward the booth.

"Yes, sir," he said. "Excuse me. What'll I do, Inspector?"

"You will stay here until relieved. I'm going upstairs. Don't let anyone come down here except the doctor and headquarters men." He turned to Nels. "You better get back on your job," he said. "When'll you be through for the night?"

"I've got to make the rounds of the whole house, from top to bottom, as soon as the audience gets out, Inspector. Then I go back to the engine house, until 9 o'clock in the morning."

"Come ahead, then. And, Officer, don't touch that booth, or let anybody touch the body until the doctor comes. If that fellow wants another nickel, give it to him, but don't let him out of the booth. There's two pieces of newspaper on that telephone book over on the table. Hands off that, too."

Nels followed the inspector up the stairs, at a respectful distance. At the first landing the big man turned on him.

"Well, Sherlock, who shot Twitchell?"

Nels stopped dead. "I don't know, Inspector," he said, earnestly.

"Neither do I. Any one of a thousand people might have a reason for rubbing him out. This'll be a headache, this case, maybe worse than the Rothstein. You don't know who shot Rothstein, do you?"

Nels shook his head.

"Then you're the only man on Broadway who'll admit he don't."

He started up the second flight.

"After you've made your rounds, come back downstairs," he instructed, dropping his voice. "Maybe you'll pick up the fellow that shot him. Did you look under the carpet?"

"No, he's not down there anywhere," said Nels, seriously. "I looked." He paused on the top step, added: "But I'll bet you I know where he is."

Maguire glared, tired of banter.

"All right, where?" he demanded.

"He's in that paper we picked up."

The inspector thought a moment.

"Maybe. But which one is it? There's fifty people in that thing. Half of 'em I never heard of. I got to find one of these wise monkeys to translate that tripe. It's all Greek to me." He turned his broad back and walked toward the exit.

Nels, making his rounds backstage, got into the big elevator at the stage floor level. In a moment it was filled with a rush of excited, chattering children in little panties and brassieres of red, white and green: luscious little fruits of the dancing school crop of last year. They got damp powder from their sweaty little cheeks and backs and arms on his blue dress coat and trod on his toes, but he only grinned. These little minxes were at least not unreal figures on a screen, even though they might be as unattainable. They were going upstairs to change for the finale, panting, tired to a frazzle, keeping up on excitement.

There was a copy of *The Evening Blade* stuck between the control box and the wall of the elevator.

"You through with that *Blade?*" the fireman asked the elevator man when the car had been emptied of its load of biological bounce and virginal vigor, on the fourth floor of the dressing room stack.

"Wanta read Twitchell?" countered the old man. "Sure. Take it. Not much in it this time, though."

"Yeah?" said the fireman. "You'd be surprised. By the way, Dad, who was it held the curtain five minutes the second act?"

Dad looked at him narrowly.

"Paris," he said.

"Who?"

"Patsy Paris. The prima ballina."

"Why?"

"She wasn't even started dressing when they called five minutes."

"What do you mean, five minutes?"

"Five minutes before the act curtain. Ain't you never been around a theatre, son?"

"Not much. Why wasn't she dressed?"

The old man glared at his impertinence. "How do I know? Ask her, why don't you, and get your face slapped." He chuckled. "No," he added, "that ain't so. She's the sweetest thing on two legs around this show, and don't you forget it. I hate to see her cryin'."

"Was she?"

"She was cryin' when I brought her down for her ballet in the second act openin'. Paul musta talked rough to her. I hear he put a fine on her for holdin' the curtain. She was still cryin' when I took her up again."

The buzzer in the car was whirring imperiously.

"Here, take the paper," said Dad, unhurried. "Maybe she had a fight with Mister Twitchell."

The fireman caught and held the door as it was sliding shut.

"What do you mean?"

The old man winked. "She's his sweetie. Watch out! I gotta go down and get them damn' boys." He went.

Nels tore out the page containing Twitchell's column and stuffed the rest of the tabloid paper into a trash can in the fourth-floor corridor. He folded the page, put it into an inside pocket and hurried on his rounds of the dressing room halls. When he arrived on the stage level again, the blues singer was out before the drop curtain, wailing while the stage was being set for the finale: the inaugural ball for the new president of San Bolivario.

Nels was wondering, as he edged around behind the plaster cyclorama of the harbor of Rio de Janeiro to get across the stage, whether he should tell Inspector Maguire about Miss Paris. A girl like that couldn't have had anything to do with killing a man. But perhaps she knew something. Look for the woman, the books said.

The detective triumphed over the gallant in Nels. He decided, on his way to the front of the house, that he'd better tell the inspector. But that would have to wait until the show was out. He had a job to do, and he'd better do it, for he was a fireman, with a couple of thousand living people to look after, and only one dead one. This detective business could wait.

Tommy Twitchell
You Don't Tell Me—

A banker insured for half a million will "fall" from a window within a week. A sacrifice fly . . . Callous Chicagoans are now calling New York the Jumping-Off Place. . . . The Lester Shipps are already on the rocks . . . Greta Land will marry Chubby as soon as his wife agrees . . . Dorothy Bardling was left waiting at the church by the voice that breathed o'er Eden Hughes and Basil Mollineaux. Constance (ex-Mollineaux) says she has no one else in mind . . . The furriers are still taking a hiding, worse this winter than last. A sepia who maids for three dizzies in the Park Plaza complains that all three of her fur coats are too shabby to wear, and no relief in sight . . . The Robert Tyre Jones, Juniors, will be storked the third time any day now . . . The Raymond Canadays (Lora Swearingen) are getting one of those chile-concarne decrees, regardless . . . The first Mrs. Cornelius Brotherton II (Cora Blaisdell) is in Reno. Into each life some blonde must fall . . . The Monte Carlo Kid

paid off in blue chips. Never kid an Okla-
homamma . . . John Drew Colt will walk on in
his mother's play in Chicago this week and
Uncle John Barrymore will wire him the tra-
ditional red apple.

Whatever became of the old-fashioned night
club? . . . The shooting and stabbing of two
men in the Club Abbey Saturday dawn will
shake Broadway's back teeth and further de-
press night club business. Filet Mignon will
be marked down to $4.95 before the winter's
over . . . Happy Carewe has been knocked for
a goal again by Mary May (née Slezak) of
the Wilde women . . . The autobiography of
what woman evangelist will not be titled
"For Goodness Sex"? . . . Old French wise-
crack I'm having carved into the head of my
bed L'amour nait de rien et meurt de tout
. . . Marya (Rubber Czech) Czerna is reviv-
ing the early American cooch dance at Chez
Jacques Jordan . . . Two Nude Nellies were
exactly that after a two-minute battle on
the floor at the Del Oro during the Headache
Hour Friday. The cause of it all gumshoed
away . . . A bright young publisher donated
$70,000 cash to the Society for the Promo-
tion of Cubist Art at a private exhibition
of rare ivory carvings Friday morning . . .

Government blasting in the East River is
giving Sutton Place the jitters. The Engi-
neers won't believe that some people must
sleep until noon. . . .

John Gant and Claire Rivoli will consolidate as soon as the lawyers draw up the title
guarantee . . . Rita Ahearn believed in Santa
Klauss and he gave her that pearl dog collar . . . Emanuel (Big Manny) Murillo never
heard of the other one in the paint racket
until he saw a newspaper headline "Murillo
bought for $285,000 by Chicago Collector."
He wanted to shoot the city editor, so the
story goes . . . That New York-Chicago gangland merger is in the air again, even though
Murillo says he came East just to see the
wife dance . . . The lofty Constance (Camera Shy) Crane was a stock ingenue in Birmingham six years ago . . . Add Hundred Most
Needless Cases: She was one of the best paid
nudes on view along Anatomical Alley. She
married her press agent and he objected to
her appearing That Way. Now they are both
out of a job . . . Alice de Kosla, back unex-
pectedly from Paris, went straight to Reno
via Westport . . . John F. (Big Chief) Curry
is Havana bound . . . Genial Gene Mahoney
announces four plays for this season to be

added to those he didn't show last year ... A Broadway spiritualist is a producer who is always communing with the angels.

Manfred Wagenaar took his toothbrush and 'cello back to the first frau—who was at least a good cook—leaving Lucia Morena to play her piano solo . . . Bruno the Basque Bruiser wears lavender underpretties, the big pansy . . . The Alpert-Torres rummance went dry ... What three former New York justices are now doormen at Foxy's Theatre? . . . Sign in a Broadway jeweler's window! Buy Now and Save Me . . . Riverside Drive is strewn with the wreckage of wren's nests that the Blizzard of 1930 blew down ... Eggs are lower than they have been in twenty years. This is a friendly warning to Rudy . . . Peggy Royce is writing another autobiography; she read her first one and didn't like the plot ... Add Hollywood lexicon! Giraffe—a silent star who will never make a sound . . . Karyl Wilde never had a sandwich named after him because no chef can design one to sell for $6.60.

What former check-room girl is in the Social Register ? . . . Hazel (Dammie) Dameron of "Night After Night" tells everybody within earshot that she is quality folks from the Eastern Shore but doesn't want it known ... Lorna Boone, the blonde in "Kiss Me Anyway" got a black marble bathtub with silver faucets from her friend, who is in plumbing ... Caroline Clayton has a Dobermann-Pinscher pup but can't spell it. She first told the donor that she couldn't accept an imported car from a practical stranger and now he rates her as a wit ... Alberta Nash says she will never give him a divorce ... It will be hotly denied, but there is still some trading going on in Wall Street ... Lisbeth Lansing calls her beloved the unemployed apple of her eye.

Rx For Boredom: Maurice Chevalier in person at the Paramount ... Jimmy (Schnozzle) Durante singing Sid Skolsky's ditty "My Broadway" at the Silver Slipper ... The minute steaks at the Stork Club, which are a blessed event. ... Those main stems that you see near the Times Bldg, when the wind is blowing. ... And "Hard Lines," a book of Rhymes-That-Don't by Ogden Nash. ... I died laughing.

3

Six men of the Homicide Squad came up from the West 20th Street Station. Obeying the telephoned instructions of Inspector Maguire, their car, its siren silent, turned into the narrow street that runs behind the New Netherland, and parked opposite the carriage entrance adjoining the stage door. A policeman stationed at that door admitted them, and they tiptoed behind the standees at the rear of the auditorium and downstairs to the lounge level without distracting the audience from the glamourous finale of the musical comedy. That was at 12:15 a.m.

At 12:20 the final curtain went down on Wilde's new hit. By 12:30 the audience was all out, ushers with flashlights were going through the rows of seats looking for lost articles. Presently only a single bulb on a movable stand on the stage floor illuminated the gloomy auditorium.

At 12:35 a.m. the medical examiner arrived, accompanied by a reporter of the City News Association who goes along to carry his bag and bottles and tip off the newspapers to good, fat murders. The doctor had been detained by a casual killing in a waterfront speakeasy down on West Street. The camera man of the Homicide Squad came in with him, carrying his heavy kit.

At 12:38 a bulletin, triple-spaced to show its importance, was clacking over the tickers of the New York City

News Association and galvanizing copy boys in all the morning newspaper offices of New York. Night editors were hastily being called in from the staff thirst parlors by their excited lieutenants.

NYCNA—13A
BULLETIN
COLUMNIST MURDERED
THE BODY OF A MAN IDENTIFIED AS THOMAS CARY TWITCHELL, COLUMNIST FOR AN EVENING NEWSPAPER (EDITORS: THE N. Y. EVENING BLADE) WAS DISCOVERED LAST (MON.) EVENING IN A TELEPHONE BOOTH IN THE NEW NETHERLAND THEATRE WHILE AN AUDIENCE OF TWO THOUSAND WAS VIEWING A NEW MUSICAL COMEDY'S PREMIERE.
(MORE)

(MGA-CA-12:38 a)

NYCNA—14A
ADD TWITGHELL MURDER
HE HAD BEEN SHOT TO DEATH
THE WEAPON WAS NOT FOUND AND NO TRACE OF THE SLAYER
INSPECTOR BARNEY J. MAGUIRE OF THE HOMICIDE SQUAD HAPPENED TO BE IN THE THEATRE AND IMMEDIATELY ASSUMED CHARGE OF THE INVESTIGATION.
(MORE)

(MGA-CA-12:39 a)

By 12:45 there were already half a dozen reporters in the lobby of the New Netherlands barred from the auditorium and the lounge beneath by policemen on post at the inner doors. The inspector would talk to them in a few minutes, he said.

At 12:49 Karyl Wilde, the eminent producer, was called out of the box office by his general publicity director, all atwitter because the newspaper boys were insisting that Tommy Twitchell was dead, downstairs. The general publicity director had been working in his office on the ninth floor, getting up, with the aid of the Social Register, a list of the more respectable celebrities in the audience to send to the society editors; he hadn't even known that anyone had been shot. He told a profane city editor on the telephone that he could give out nothing to the press without consulting Mr. Wilde. So he scrambled down nine flights of stairs in the dark and met the shock troops of the press in the lobby.

Mr. Wilde in the box office was telling a newspaper man on the telephone:

"I really don't know anything about it. The poor fellow was shot in a telephone booth downstairs just as my audience was leaving my show. It was unfortunate, but of course my staff couldn't prevent it. We were able to send my audience home without any knowledge of the tragedy to mar their perfect enjoyment of my new hit, *Rebel Rose,* which is sold out for months in spite of this ticket combine which has been trying to strangle me and my productions. I'll issue a statement on it later." He hung up.

There was no logical reason for Wilde's deceiving the press, but habit is strong. He told the agitated press agent to invite the boys up to his office to have a drink. The boys insisted they must see Inspector Maguire first. Mr. Wilde stayed in the box office. He would have to issue a bull reassuring the public that no more patrons would be permitted to be killed in the washroom or the telephone booths or anywhere in the theatre during the run of rebel rose, which should endure at least two years on Broadway. He called in the unhappy press agent again, and dictated a statement to be telegraphed to all city editors at once. It ran to 500 words and ended with a glowing tribute to the personal character of Mr. Twitchell, whatever his professional ethics might be. This, Mr. Wilde felt sincerely, should be worth a box in anybody's paper, and should be carried on the national press wires. The press agent tiptoed off upstairs to put the statement into English.

When Nels Lundberg came back downstairs at 12:45 a.m., the tall, lean, serious medical examiner was standing at the foot of the staircase. A flare from one of those safety bulb flashlights blinded the fireman: the police photographer was taking pictures of the body as it had been found in the booth, before the doctor made a detailed examination.

A dapper detective walked over to Nels.

"You the fireman that found him?" he asked. Nels nodded assent.

"Was he just like that when you first saw him?"

Nels went around to the booth, verified that fact and came back.

"The guy that shot him must'a stuffed him into the booth. I suppose a dozen of you put your prints on that door handle?" the detective continued.

"Only me and maybe the colored porter. We had to get him out to see if he was dead. He was still bleeding."

"Sure. Can't be helped. But he certainly didn't close that door on himself."

"How do you figure that?"

"The bullet didn't go through the glass nor through the door panels, but it's lodged in the top back corner of the booth, near the right side. Small caliber. About a .25." He was talking more to the grave-faced doctor than to Nels. "You range that slug back through his head and chin and it proves he was standing in front of the open booth when the shot was fired with the gun right up under his chin. He was turned a little to his left and his heels were almost against the sill of the booth."

The doctor lighted a cigarette and strolled away.

"Did you dig out the bullet?" Nels asked.

"No. We'll take the whole booth apart and put it on ice for the trial."

"Who you going to try?" asked Nels, innocently.

The detective snorted and walked away. Two men were measuring the hall floor with a steel tape. Nels looked into the smoking lounge. Nobody there. Where was Inspector Maguire? At this moment a captain and a sergeant, in uniform, came down the stairs. From the precinct, they'd be.

Inspector Maguire was following them down, alongside a fine figure of a man who was carrying a long black opera cape, folded to show its baby blue lining, and one of those trick hats, pancaked shut, on one arm, and a black overcoat and black velour hat on the other. The man had red hair, and his unmistakably Irish face was vaguely familiar to Nels.

"Oh, Alex, come over here," the inspector called across the hallway. A man of about thirty, very good looking in a rugged way, dressed in heather-mixture tweeds, brown brogues, and a green felt hat, turned from the telephone directory table over which he had been bent, and came briskly across.

"This is Shane O'Neal, the singer, Alex. Sergeant Rorty of the Broadway detail, Shane. Mr. O'Neal came with Twitchell tonight and he's been waiting upstairs, with his hat and coat."

"Where is he?" O'Neal asked, huskily, his face dead-white. "Did they take him away?"

"Not for a couple of hours, yet," said Maguire. "The Commissioner is on his way over, Alex. Tell the boys he's coming."

"The body's in the telephone booth, where they found it," Rorty answered O'Neal's question. "The photographer's still working on it."

"Didn't anybody hear the shot?" O'Neal demanded, in the same low, forced tone. "They might have saved his life—"

"Not a chance," Maguire declared. "He was drilled right through the brain from here to here." He indicated with his forefingers the spots under his chin and above and behind his left ear where the bullet had entered and emerged. "He couldn't have lived a minute, I'd say."

O'Neal clutched at Rorty's arm. The fireman, hovering behind them, caught him. They supported him through the archway and laid him on the divan at its left. When Nels returned with a paper cup of ice water, O'Neal had opened his eyes.

"I'm sorry, Barney," he said, weakly, after he had gulped the water. "The shock was too much for me. I never could stand the sight of blood, you'll maybe remember. And Tommy was my closest friend in the world." He sat up, buried his face in his hands.

"Shane grew up down on Avenue A," Maguire spoke in a low voice to Rorty. "I've known him since he was a shaver; I knew his old man well."

"How about any other close friends? Did Twitchell have any?" Rorty asked. "If you feel like talking now, Mr. O'Neal, you can be a lot of help to us."

"I'm all right." The baritone passed a hand, covered with fine red hairs, across his eyes, shook his head vigorously, leaned back against the divan, and spoke, slowly, his voice trembling. "Why, no, Tommy had few really close friends. I suppose you could say Wylie King and I were the only real intimates—and Edwards, his publisher, though Mr. Edwards doesn't know him as well as we do. God, I can't believe this!"

"I know King very well," said the inspector, trying to stay off emotional ground. "He'll be just the lad to help us. Look here, Shane: I found—this fireman found it—a page torn out of the *Blade* and then torn in two like somebody had snatched at it."

"I was looking at it, around there," Rorty cut in. "Where'd you find it, chief?"

"One piece, crumpled up, on the floor right there." He indicated the spot beyond the tall Chinese dragon jar that stood between the end of the divan and the archway. "Somebody had balled it up and thrown it at the jar and missed his aim. The other piece, that wasn't crumpled— the top part of the page—was in the booth under his feet, like he had dropped it when he collapsed."

"But what's the significance of that?" O'Neal demanded, puzzled.

"Didn't I tell you? It was Twitchell's page from this afternoon's paper, with all the dirt of Broadway in it."

"Yes, I see," O'Neal said, slowly.

"My friend here," Maguire indicated Nels with his thumb, "thinks the clue that will solve the case is in the column. The trouble is that there's fifty-seven people named or mentioned in it."

Rorty shook his head, gloomily. "The tipoff's just as likely to be in a column printed last week or last month or last year, if it's in a column at all. One thing, Inspector: I'd take the fireman's hunch seriously enough to go over the back files of Twitchell's stuff."

"On the other hand, Alex," said the inspector, pulling at his upper lip. "Don't it seem more likely that somebody would get burned up by this item today—whichever it was—and come gunning for Twitchell? The longer a person waits, the less likely he is to take the risk of shooting a man. And in a public place like this! Only a crazy man would do it. He got out, sure—but the chances were 99 to

1 against him. If he laid plans ahead to get Twitchell, he wouldn't 'a planned to get him here. I think it's a ten-to-one shot this fellow was crazy mad, and didn't give a damn what happened to him."

"Why a man, necessarily?" O'Neal spoke up. "Why not a woman? Doesn't a woman shoot before she thinks?"

"Near always," said Maguire. "There's sense in what you say, Shane. But the first thing we've got to do is to get that gibberish translated into police English. Can you do it, Alex?"

"The slang is plain enough to me. What I don't know is some of the—what's the word?"

"The innuendo?" O'Neal supplied.

"That's it. I'm on Broadway duty two years, now, but I don't know half these people he mentions. He's got Park Avenue and Wall Street and gangland and Hollywood and even the other side of the pond in it. You'd do better at it than I would, Mr. O'Neal."

"There's one man who could do better at it than Tommy, himself," said O'Neal. His voice was stronger, now.

"Who's that?"

"Wylie King."

"To be sure. To be sure," said Maguire. "In another week I'd 'a thought of him, myself. Where'll he be at the moment?"

"He was here, but I saw him leave right after the second act started. At least he went up the aisle and didn't come back."

"Did he have his hat and coat, did you notice?"

"No, I think not. I'm sure not. I suppose he checked them."

"Why didn't Twitchell check his, do you know?"

"It's a newspaperman's habit to keep his hat and coat by him in the theatre. Don't ask me why. I didn't check mine because he kept his."

"They don't like to tip," said Rorty. "It would cost 'em a pile of money, with all the gyp joints they go into in a year's work."

"But where can we get King?" Maguire cut in.

"I'd try his apartment, first. Here's the number of his private line." O'Neal brought out his address book, opened it, handed it over. "I'm not up to breakin' the news to him, myself."

"I'll talk to him," said Maguire. "I'll tell him to come over here and we'll all put our heads together on this column. Who's got a nickel?"

Nels had one left.

"My Man Friday," said the Inspector. He clapped Nels on the shoulder. "How'd you like to work for me, fireman?"

"I sure would," said Nels, earnestly.

"The hell you would!" Maguire roared. "All the firemen want to be cops and all the cops know damn well they'd rather be firemen. You don't know your luck, boy."

"I'd like to be a detective," Nels insisted, flushing.

"Well, what else are ye now?" The inspector started toward the booths by the ladies' room door.

"Look here, Barney!" O'Neal got up. "You'll be wanting to go through Tommy's apartment, I suppose?"

"Sure. I was going to take Alex, and do that as soon as the Commissioner got here."

"Well, why not talk to Wylie over there? He lives in the building, you know. And he'll likely be undressed if he's at home. You'll save time."

"What building?"

"The Park Tower. I live there, too. Tommy has one penthouse apartment and I've the other. Wylie lives down on the twelfth floor."

"You're feeling all right, Shane?"

"I am, thank you." He got to his feet. "Look here, Barney, there'll be a mob of reporters storming this place. I don't feel like facing them tonight. I'd like to go home. If you'll come along, we'll get Wylie over there and go to work. For one thing, I need a shot of good whiskey."

Maguire considered. "Why not?" he decided. He went on into a booth. They heard his big voice booming. Apparently he had found his man. He came out presently, mopping perspiration.

"I think I hear the Commissioner around on the other side. Wait a minute." He disappeared through the archway.

O'Neal was walking up and down now, Rorty and the fireman watching him.

"Second time I ever fainted in me life," he apologized. "The first time was when a lad got run down by a ferry boat whilst we were swimmin'. I was out of me head for two days."

"I don't enjoy these sights, myself," Rorty assured him. "The oldest man on the force will get faint, sometimes, at what he's got to see. Kids under street cars are the worst."

"You ought to be in the fire department," offered Nels, grimly.

Maguire came thudding back. He addressed Rorty.

"The Commissioner says to drop everything and follow this up wherever it takes me. I'm taking you to help me, Alex. It's likely to take us a long time and a far ways, I'm thinkin'. Now we'll go over to the Park Tower. I hope the reporters ain't got there first."

"They'd never get up to Tommy's place," Shane assured them. "One thing we insist on and get is privacy and protection. The downstairs staff can't be tied in New York. One slip, and out the man goes."

"Ye must have bad consciences," Maguire said. "Let's go."

Nels saw his detective career ending right there. He plucked at the inspector's sleeve.

"There's something I found out backstage that I ought to tell you, Inspector."

Maguire glared at him. "Well, come along, then. We're wasting time."

Nels came along. When he could get to a telephone, he'd call the watchman at the engine house and leave word he was held as a material witness by Inspector Maguire. This was a break.

They went out the rear way, into the back street. There were a couple of men watching the stage door. They came running up the sidewalk to pounce on Maguire.

"I've got nothing to add to what I gave the City News," Maguire assured the reporters. "That's straight, boys. We have no clue yet to the murderer." He walked on, and addressed Rorty as they reached the sidewalk.

"The first thing you can do, Alex, is go around the corner and get three or four copies of that paper. We'll pick you up."

"It'll be hard to find any around here this late," Rorty warned him.

Nels brought a folded page out of an inside pocket of his coat, then another.

"I got these out of the trash cans, backstage," he said.

"Ha—the fire department!" Maguire boomed out. "All right, they'll do."

A bitter wind was blowing from the northwest. Maguire herded them into a car at the curb. Nels got in beside the driver.

"It's Inspector Haley's," Maguire explained, "but he won't be needin' it until they send the body to Bellevue, anyways. Take us to the Park Tower, Mike."

O'Neal shivered. "When'll that be?"

"Not for a couple of hours, at least."

"Well," said Rorty, sighing, "this street'll go clean nuts by morning. The papers are already out with it."

Maguire, silent in the corner of the seat, now spoke up.

"What happened between Twitchell and this night club doll he used to keep?"

"Marya Czerna? He never kept her. She made her own money," O'Neal objected.

"My error. But she lived with him?"

"Nearly a year. Why, they broke up over another woman, I suppose, Barney. It's been all off between them for a couple of months."

"I could have told you that," Rorty assured the inspector.

"They didn't part friends?"

O'Neal delayed his answer, shook his head, ominously. "She tried to stab him with a paper cutter."

"Where was this?"

"In his apartment. The day after Thanksgiving."

"I thought you said nobody could get in there."

"Tommy asked her there. He wanted to make a friendly settlement."

"Did he tell you about this, himself?"

"Lord, no! I was there. I got the knife away from her. I've still got the marks across the inside of me hand and fingers."

"The hell you say! What did she want—money?"

"She wanted Tommy. That girl's a blonde wop, you know, and a hot potato."

"I thought she was a Czech," Rorty objected, "or a Bohemian. She told me she was born in Pilsen, where the beer came from."

"She was born in Bridgeport, Connecticut," said O'Neal tartly. "Her name was Maria Nera or Neri. She translated it into Czech. In English it's Mary Black."

"Like yours is Johnny Neal," said Barney, with no trace of sarcasm in his tone.

"Exactly. Artists do that to make themselves more glamourous. The public demands glamour, you know."

"Well, the public gets it from Mary, all right," said Maguire, heartily. "Twitchell must have been crazy to let a dame like that get away from him."

"Well, you see, Tommy really fell in love, about three months ago. A fine little girl. He was going to marry her."

"Who?"

There was a long silence before Shane replied.

"Barney, is there no way she could be spared all this? But I don't see how she can. No, she can't. She'll be dragged through it, no matter what I do."

He stopped, considered, came out with it:

"The girl is Patricia Paris."

"That little dancer in the show?"

"The same."

"Why, she's only a kid, Shane."

"A darlin', she is," said O'Neal, gently. "She was going to a party tonight with Tommy and me. It had gone clean out of my mind."

"That musta been who Czerna meant," Barney reflected aloud.

"Meant what?"

"Why, I saw her, coming out of the theatre about five minutes before the show broke up. I tried to talk to her, because I knew her and Twitchell had been—friends, but she couldn't stop. I says to her: 'Looking for your boy friend?' and she says: 'Which boy friend?' and I says 'Tommy' and she says 'You're damn' right, I'm looking for that bastard and you can tell him so for me!' and then she says 'Well, I gotta lam over to the club and rouge the knees and powder the tummy before the boobs get there.' And she blew. I put a man on her. We can get her any time. She's at the Del Oro now. I hear Jack Jordan bought the club from Alpert. Is that right?"

"That's right," said Rorty.

There was a silence as they were halted by a traffic light. O'Neal broke it.

"You watched the audience leave the theatre, Barney. Did you see anyone else you think might have any reason for killing Tommy?"

"How should I know? I saw a couple of dozen who would kill him or you or me, just as soon as not. Remember, Shane, I haven't been shadowing Twitchell with the idea of catching his murderer red-handed. All I've got is a list of people that was there that have got records, downtown. I had three men spotting with me, but we missed some, anyway."

The car slid into a curb and halted. A Park-Tower doorman, a giant in a sage green overcoat, opened the door.

"A cold night, Mr. O'Neal," he volunteered. Shane getting out last, didn't answer. He was still very white of face.

"We'll talk to the manager first," said Maguire. "Suppose you do that, Alex, put an officer on post in the lobby, and then join us up in Twitchell's place." He said something to the driver, who saluted and drove away.

"Let's go to my apartment first, if you don't mind," Shane suggested. "I've got a key to Tommy's and we can go in there any time you like. I want a drink."

"All right," said Maguire, curtly. Leaving Rorty in the lobby, they got into a Circassian walnut and silver elevator and were shot up past thirty-two floors to the level marked PH.

Sitting on the modernistic lounge facing the elevator doors was a man in a wine-colored silk dressing gown over his waistcoat; otherwise he was in evening dress except for wine-colored Morocco slippers. He got up.

"Wylie," said O'Neal, putting an arm around the smaller man's shoulders. "This is horrible!. Horrible!"

"I can't believe it," said King, slowly. "And yet—I'm not surprised. I told him! I told him!" He broke off to shake hands with the inspector, saying: "I'm glad you're here, Barney, and not some bigwig I don't know."

With a shaking hand, O'Neal inserted a key into the door marked PH L.

"Come in, fireman," said the host to Nels, hovering outside the door, cap in hand.

"This is Nels Lundberg, who was on duty at the theatre tonight," the inspector explained to King, who gave Nels an ice-cold hand. "He found the body, as I told you, and he picked up the pieces of Twitchell's column."

"I've got one here," said King, bringing a folded clipping out of the pocket of his dressing gown. "I was trying to analyze it while I was waiting for you. But I'm still too dazed to think straight."

O'Neal had preceded them through the entrance hall, snapping on lights as he went.

"My man has the night off," he called back. "I was going to a party at Ted Edwards' after the show."

The three of them followed the host into the baronial living room, two stories high, furnished in heavy, dark oak that looked as though it had come from an Irish castle and actually had, along with the tapestries, the paneling and the Irish harp standing beside the grand piano in a corner between two rows of heavily draped windows.

"You do yourself proud, Shane," said Maguire, heartily.

O'Neal pulled a heavy cord. Eight drapes slid back, disclosing a view northward across Central Park, with Fifth Avenue stretching away at the right and the lights of Central Park West going up the left hand of the picture framed by the four tall windows.

"Magnificent! 'Tis fair magnificent, this town," said Maguire, "when you get up high enough to see it."

"Tommy's view is even better," said Shane. "He could see all of Times Square and Broadway and his whole happy hunting grounds without even getting out of bed. All the south half of Manhattan, down to the Statue of Liberty on a clear day or night. With glasses you can watch the big ships go through the Narrows from our roof terrace. Will you gentlemen take chairs, and I'll get something for the good of us all."

He disappeared through a doorway hung with tapestry. If a fire ever got started in here, Nels thought, running his eye over the hangings, he'd be out a pretty penny. They seated themselves, Maguire in a massive carved chair near the piano, the fireman in a straight-backed one near the huge fireplace, and King on the piano bench. Even the piano had been finished to appear centuries old.

"What has developed since you talked to me, Barney?" King began.

"Not much. The Commissioner, himself, is there and the Chief Inspector, and most of my Homicide Squad."

"I wondered," said King. "When I called Ted Edwards he hadn't heard a word from his office—"

"You called Edwards, did you?" Maguire cut in, sharply.

"You didn't tell me not to. He's Tommy's employer, and he was the first man I thought of."

"I believe Twitchell and Shane were going to a party there after the show with this Miss Paris."

King looked hard at the inspector.

"Who told you that, Barney?"

"O'Neal. He wanted to keep her out of it, too, but man, you can't! Where is she? I'll be wanting to talk to her presently."

"She was to meet them at Ted's. It's only four blocks from here, on Park Avenue."

"Was she there when you talked to Edwards?"

"No. He's going to break the news to her and bring her over here to talk to me. And to you, of course, Barney."

There was an uncomfortable silence.

"They'll be along any minute. I told the doorman to send them right up," King added.

A telephone bell whirred somewhere just as the host came in with a tray of bottles, glasses and a siphon. He set the tray on a coffee table by the fireplace, went over to the south wall, pulled back a tapestry and took out a one-hand instrument.

"Toss a match under the logs in the fireplace, will you, Wylie. I feel cold. Yes, what is it?"

Nels obliged. The fire began to crackle up through the kindling and the cedar logs.

"Why, yes," O'Neal was saying. "Surely. Well, I'm sorry you had so much trouble. House rules, you know, not to call us on the telephone. Hold the line—Inspector, here's one of your men."

The inspector crossed over and took the telephone. They could hear him saying "Yes . . . yes. . . . All right. . . . When's her next show? . . . All right, ask her to come over to the Park Tower with you right away and see me. . . . We'll be in Shane O'Neal's apartment or else Twitchell's, in the penthouse. . . . Don't be rough now, but get her here. . . . Tell her she can get back in time for the next show, sure. Don't tell her a word about the killing."

Another buzzer was sounding.

"That's the door," said O'Neal. "Wylie, you be bartender, will you? No more for me just now. I had a shot in the pantry." He went out through the hallway to the foyer. As Inspector Maguire replaced the house telephone behind the tapestry, Sergeant Rorty came in, followed by O'Neal. Rorty threw his hat and overcoat on the chair which held the inspector's derby and Chesterfield.

"There's a bunch of the maddest star reporters I ever saw downstairs," said Rorty, grinning. "It's all the doorman and the elevator boys can do to keep 'em from taking the place by storm. They all say they knew Twitchell and think that ought to get 'em into his rooms. They've got 'em sitting in the lobby out of the cold, but not a man Jack can come up to Twitchell's unless you say the word, Inspector. I got a cop in off the street to take their cussin' in the name of the department. Two of them are trying to phone the Commissioner."

"Good Lord!" Wylie King groaned. "I don't want them waylaying Patsy when she comes in. Maybe I'd better go down and talk to them, Barney."

"They were asking for you. The boys told 'em you were out. They were asking for Mr. O'Neal, too."

"How'd you get away from 'em?" Wylie quizzed.

"I ducked through the manager's office and came up in the service elevator," Rorty explained.

Another buzzer was whirring. O'Neal started, spilled the whiskey he was pouring for the late arrival.

"Will you answer it, Wylie?" he pleaded. "I'm shaking like a leaf. It's the outside phone, the private line. The gold one, you know."

King got the gold one out from behind the tapestry. The rest listened.

"This is Wylie," he said. "No, Ted, I haven't seen her. . . . But my God, man—Are you sure? . . . Come on over here. . . . We'll have to get organized before we start. . . . Well, if she comes here, she'll be sent right up. I'll go downstairs. and leave instructions. We don't want her running into all the reporters. . . . Well, get over here as soon as you can. Go to the service entrance on the side street and I'll have a boy waiting to bring you up the back way. . . . Right. . . ."

King fumbled the instrument back into place behind the tapestry.

"What's that about Patsy?" O'Neal demanded.

"Ted got her when she came in, and before she took off her coat, he took her into his bedroom and told her. He said she took it without a whimper, with just her lips moving. She asked only one question: 'Are you sure he's dead?'"

King stopped, cleared his throat shatteringly. Every man in the room was on his feet.

"He went out to tell his guests that he had to leave the party. When he came back to the bedroom, Patsy was gone."

"Where, for God's sake?" O'Neal exploded.

"Down the elevator. Some people coming to the party said she got in as they got out. The doorman said she ran west, toward Madison Avenue, on foot. Ted's been trying to find me for the last fifteen minutes."

A telephone bell whirred. Wylie spun around.

"The house phone," said O'Neal, dully.

"No, but hold the line," King said into it. "Barney, it's for you again."

Maguire got up and went across. His conversation was again a series of "Yes . . . yes . . ." Then his voice rose. "You're a hell of a cop!" he exploded. "Well, don't alibi me. . . . What's that . . . Hello! Hello!"

Maguire turned to the waiting group.

"This boy I put on Marya Czerna let her get out of the club while he was talkin' to me, before. Now he can't find her. . . . And just as I'm about to take the stripes off him, some kind of a riot starts in the club."

"What was it?" chorused Rorty and King.

"I'm holdin' the line while this bonehead finds out. The next he knows, Jack Jordan's gang will be stealin' his gun right out of his holster."

"Jordan owns the Del Oro now," King commented. "The grapes must have paid him plenty."

"I hear he's Czerna's new papa," Rorty put in.

King shrugged. Rorty went on:

"They say he moved right in after Tommy moved out. I don't know, though. She's sunk about Tommy. I think maybe she's just been giving Jordan a lot of promissory notes—or took up with him as a defiance of Tommy. By golly, do you know that gives me an idea. . . ."

Maguire shushed them. "I couldn't hear," he said into the telephone. "Say that again. . . . Well, who is she? . . .

Well, for cripe's sake go back and find out! You haven't got the sense you was born with, tonight."

Another wait.

"Some dame just took a shot at Jack Jordan in his office at the Del Oro," Maguire reported, fuming.

They were all on their feet, waiting. O'Neal began to pace distractedly back and forth across the great hearthrug, his hands clasped behind the tails of his dress coat.

"The thing to do while we're waiting for Mr. Edwards to get here," said Maguire, still holding the telephone, "is to take that column of Twitchell's apart and find out what's behind all the dirt he printed yesterday. The fireman's got a couple of copies. You two gentlemen and you, Alex, be lookin' it over. We're wastin' a lot of time. I think I'll hang up and let that sap call me up when he finds out something. . . . Yes. . . . All right, spill it. . . . *What?* . . . Did she hit him? . . . No, *don't take her to the station.* . . . *Bring her over here to me.* . . . That's what I said. Wait, now. Where's Jordan? . . . Oh, they did . . . and where was you? . . . All right. . . . Never mind. . . . Bring her on. . . . Pick up the first man you see and tell him to go after Jordan. . . . I'll notify the precinct. . . . That's all. . . . Tell her Mr. King and Mr. O'Neal are here and want to help her. Don't be rough, now, but don't let her get away or you'll be patrolin' Staten Island tomorrow."

King and O'Neal were at Maguire's side now.

Maguire let his arm drop and stood with the instrument against his black silk vest. There was dull amazement in his face when he spoke:

"Your friend Miss Paris shot Jack Jordan. He don't know how bad. They got him away too quick."

4

"It can't be Patsy!"

King and O'Neal confronted the inspector angrily, as though challenging him to prove it.

Maguire freed his right arm from King's grip and replaced the telephone instrument in the niche behind the tapestry.

"I don't think there's any mistake," he assured them. "Reed said it was Patricia Paris, the dancer in Wilde's show."

"Who told him it was?" King demanded.

"She told him."

"But it couldn't be," O'Neal protested. "She wouldn't shoot a man. And why should she shoot Jordan?"

"No woman would shoot a man, Shane, but some of them do. We'll find out when Reed gets here with her."

King threw out his hands in a gesture of helplessness and slumped down on the divan that faced the fireplace a dozen feet from the hearthrug. He looked very small on the leather couch, of a massiveness to suit this high-ceilinged room that represented to the Irish baritone the departed glory of his ancestors.

"Heirlooms of the Clan O'Neal," Wylie called the furniture, "every one made to order." But the effect, even in a penthouse thirty-three floors above mid-Manhattan looking out across Central Park, was quite worth the effort. Draw the heavy draperies across the tall leaded windows so as to shut out the aerial map of the city, and the interior of this apartment, cooperatively owned by O'Neal and finished to his architect's and decorator's specifications, might pass for a portion of an Irish castle with modern improvements.

The owner of this magnificence sat down heavily on the carved bench at the piano at the right of the open space before the hearth and leaned forward, chafing his hands between his knees, miserably.

"Now, gentlemen," said the inspector, "I know you're upset. But she'll come to no harm. Let's go at this column of Twitchell's and try to make some sense of it." He turned to the fireman, standing near the telephone. "Let's have one of those papers, son, and give one to the sergeant."

Nels passed over the pages he had torn from two copies of the *Blade*. Mr. King drew his clipping from a pocket of his dressing gown and unfolded it.

O'Neal went over and sat down by him on the divan, to share the clipping.

"Get out your book, Alex," the inspector instructed, putting on a pair of the new-fangled full vision spectacles which made him look more Jovian still. Sergeant Rorty moved a tall back chair around so he could rest his notebook on the end of the grand piano and still face the others. King got up, crossed to an antique oaken desk in the corner by the windows and brought back to the divan a tooled leather blotting pad, some sheets of stationery and a patent pencil.

"I'll take some notes, too, if you don't mind, Barney," he said. The inspector nodded assent, cleared his throat, seated himself heavily in a leather-covered armchair between the divan and the fireplace.

"Now suppose we take just the items that mention people or that we think might have a bearing on the murder."

He read out, in the uncertain inflections of one to whom reading aloud is still a grammar school task:

"'A banker insured for half a million will "fall" from a window within a week. A sacrifice fly. Callous Chicagoans are calling New York the Jumping-Off Place. . . .' That's a hell of an item! Who's the banker?"

Neither King nor O'Neal could enlighten him. "It's probably a joke of Tommy's," said King.

Maguire grunted. "What's this about the Lester Shipps being on the rocks?"

"English actor, in the movies. Long Island society wife. Too much Hollywood."

"Are we going too fast for you, Sergeant?" King asked Rorty.

"I write a kind of shorthand of my own," said the detective. "I'll holler if you get too speedy."

King answered the question:

"Greta Land was a dancer, first on Broadway, and then in the silent pictures. She can't get rid of her accent, and she lisps, anyway. She's playing this young Chalfonte, the son of the Amalgamated Alloys president. His wife was one of the Ellerton girls: Philadelphia family, lots of jack and swank, but homely as a mudhen. She'll go to Reno, I suppose. They've been married about five years and separated about a year."

Rorty put in: "I see this Greta Land around the night clubs a lot with him, I guess it is. Young looking but clean bald, and roly-poly?" King nodded assent. "Well, she certainly ain't homely. I get dizzy looking at her."

"You're on the Broadway detail, Alex, just to look at dizzy dames," said the inspector, drily. "Do your duty, no matter how much you hurt your eyes. Now, who are these people in the next one?"

O'Neal supplied that information. Basil Mollineaux, he explained, was a young blood who hung around the

American bars in Paris and the beach resorts and casinos
in France, mostly. His wife was one of the Taillor girls.
He had married her about six years back and had tried to
settle down, but he and Constance didn't get along well.
Eden Hughes had been a Mrs. Waldo, from Boston; Basil
had met her overseas. She had gone to Reno after coming home and Basil had married her on last Friday in San
Francisco, right after she was divorced. Dorothy Bardling
was a divorcee of the Hamptons set, who would have been
named as co-respondent if Constance had got her divorce
in New York, instead of Paris.

"Tommy used to know Mollineaux when he lived
abroad," he concluded.

"The way these swells marry and unmarry makes me
dizzy," said Maguire.

"Then, as I get it, Mollineaux and his wife are on the
Coast. Where's his ex-wife?" Rorty asked.

"Somewhere abroad. Probably Egypt. You might check
that up. Dorothy Bardling was here; I saw her at the Wilde
opening last night."

"So did I," said King. "She was taking a razzing from
her alleged friends in the lobby. That woman can curse
like a stable groom. And when she's tight she does."

"If she was going to be laughed at, why did she show
herself?" Maguire asked.

"In her set you don't let on that you give a damn,
unless you're accused of a serious crime like cheating at
cards," said King, smiling. "But they got under her hide
with their kidding."

"Do you think it's likely that she'd shoot Twitchell?"

"Most unlikely," said King. O'Neal nodded his agreement.

"You know her personally?"

"Shane could have been her next husband," said King,
winking.

"Not while I'm conscious," Shane growled.

"She was using foul language about the deceased just prior to the murder. Get all that, Alex?" Rorty nodded.

"Don't let that weigh too heavily," said O'Neal "It's nothing unusual in her gang. They're all tough as a boot."

"I can remember the day," said Maguire, grimly, "when a lady was a lady, or else— You do well to look up a dame in the Social Register now before you pull her for drunk and disorderly. Well, the Commissioner can have the pleasure of talking to Mrs. Bardling. Next item."

"Skip the gag about fur coats and the Bobby Jones stork item. The next one simply means that the Canadays are getting one of those Mexican mail-order divorces in spite of the ruling of some New York judge that they don't hold in this state."

"No cause for shooting there?" Maguire suggested.

"Unlikely," said King.

"'The first Mrs. Cornelius Brotherton II (Cora Blaisdell) is in Reno. Into each life some blonde must fall.'" Maguire read out. "Who's the blonde?"

"I don't know her name; I never saw her before tonight, but she's certainly a hot cha-cha." King assured him. "She was at the show with Brotherton. They were so fatuous about each other they didn't even look at the stage. Cross them off."

"Who's Brotherton's wife?"

"One of the army and navy set in Washington. She's probably got her next husband all picked out, anyway. They take the fortunes of war with good grace."

"Well, better luck to the blonde," said O'Neal.

"Who's this Monte Carlo Kid who paid off the Oklahoma—what the hell is that word?"

"Oklahoma mamma," King explained. "It's Harvey Thatcher. He fell heir to a lot of Oklahoma oil money and went into picture producing. His first picture was called

Wheels. It was laid in Monte Carlo mostly, though it was about Americans. Grandfather made a small fortune out of bicycles, father made a whopping one out of automobiles, and the only son spends it and loses it at roulette. They took the company to Detroit and Monte Carlo, spent two millions on the silent version and left most of it on the cutting room floor when the talkies came in. Harvey retook it with sound and it's cleaning up like ammonia all over the country. He's got the laugh on everybody who called him Wheels. The new nickname is the Monte Carlo Kid—he picked it himself."

"I saw the picture," said Rorty. "It was swell."

"Well," King resumed, "Thatcher now wants to marry his baby-faced leading woman. But there was a hot mamma from Muskogee who had first call on him. She showed up in New York just before *Wheels* opened on Broadway last week and put a six-shooter in Harvey's teeth. She was all for being made an honest woman, but the lawyers talked her around and sent her to Europe to spend it. She sailed Friday midnight. That lets her out, I suppose. But Thatcher was at the Wilde show, with his sweetie."

"You seem to know a lot about it, Wylie," Maguire remarked. "Did you tell Twitchell?"

"Yes, and if you tell anybody I told you, Barney, I'll have to call you a liar. In picture business we never offend the angels; you can't tell when you may need one."

"All this is confidential between us," said Maguire, reassuringly. "But I think we'd better follow up this Thatcher. Them Oklahoma boys are touchy. The next is some kind of a gag. We'll skip this item about the Abbey Club, and go into it later. I didn't handle that case. We don't know much yet on it. Let's see. . . . Happy Carewe is the drunk lad who was down in the lounge and talked to you after you found the body, ain't he, fireman?"

"That's who Mr. Wilde and Mr. Flaxon said he was," the fireman replied, cautiously. "But I don't think he would kill anybody."

"How can you tell?"

Nels shrugged his shoulders. "Maybe I can't."

"I agree with him," King put in. "Happy's a fine boy, of his sort; generous, honest, just a kid, though he's past thirty. He'd make an ideal king for any Balkan country with a sense of humor."

"Then this wouldn't make him sore?"

"Lord, no! Happy's been falling in love with the chorus ever since he was in prep school. He's a godsend to tired chorus girls. When he sobers up and reads that item he'll send Tommy a box of cigars—" King broke off, realizing that Tommy would never smoke another cigar with him, downstairs in King's book-lined room, up here in the rooms just through that wall. Seeing the pain through the little man's sardonic mask, Nels tried to relieve it.

"I lent him a penny tonight to get a water cup and he said he was going to send me a box of cigars with a penny in the top," he said, in his slow careful English.

Mr. King managed a smile. "I got him out of a jam with a Follies girl once and he sent me a box with a thousand-dollar bill in it. They weren't my kind of cigars and I gave them to the elevator starter in the Ponderous Building. In five minutes the starter came up, white as a sheet, and handed me the bill."

"A break for you," said Rorty, enviously.

"I sent it back to Happy with a note saying: 'You'll need this to get yourself into another jam. Don't mention it.' And we've been pretty good friends ever since."

"Well, we won't bother him unless we have to," said Maguire. "This item about Marya Czerna seems to be the next with a name in it. But how about this fight at the Del

Oro Club. That's what he means by the Chez Jack Jordan, I suppose."

"I know about that," O'Neal spoke up. "Tommy thought it was so funny that he came around by the terrace and told me about it—we've got keys to each other's terrace doors. The press agent for the Del Oro had just phoned him about it."

"When was that?"

"A little after two o'clock Friday morning. I had just come in from a party. Tommy could see my lights on the terrace from his office in there. He was writing this column then. I went in and had a drink with him, and he told me about this fracas. The fellow is an overshoe manufacturer from Ohio. There's a little Armenian dancer in the Del Oro floor show who calls herself Tanya—she's been playing him. Another of the little nudes was standing close to him and he pinched her and this Tanya dived across the floor, tore into her and ripped off her lifebelt with the first grab. The other one snatched off Tanya's and they rolled all over the floor as naked as they were born. Everybody had a big time until Jordan gave his muscle men the sign to stop it. He held up this Tanya's hand like a prizefight winner's and proposed they put on a return match during the next show, but there was a plainclothes man in the house and he told Jordan to lay off; it was too rough. So Marya Czerna took up a collection to buy the poor little girls some bungalow aprons and got nearly a hundred dollars for them. The gumshoe king had made a quick sneak while the fight was on."

"Well, they wouldn't shoot a man for printing that, I guess," Maguire said, grinning. "You say Twitchell wrote this column Friday morning? As early as that?"

"That was his custom," said O'Neal. "He'd write what he had for Monday between about three o'clock and dawn on Friday, usually, and put in later items up to Sunday about 6 p.m., when the syndicate wire had to have the last of it. This week he said he was getting it up early, because he was going out to Greenport, Long Island, for the week end."

"Who with?"

"He didn't say. Tommy kept up his connections with the society crowd. They amused him and he got some juicy items that way."

"So he had society connections?" Maguire appeared to be surprised.

"Didn't you know that?"

"As I said before, Shane, the department hasn't made a special study of Twitchell though I see now we should have." A smile drew the sting from Maguire's remark. "What about his, eh—background?"

O'Neal looked at King, on his right. Wylie answered the question.

"Well, he wasn't exactly born in the Four Hundred, but he grew up on the fringes of it. His father was Dr. Arthur Hadley Twitchell, down in Washington Square. One of the old silk hat school, with a smart carriage trade. Heidelburg graduate, and the descendant of English gentry. He was a widower—the wife died when Tommy was about four. The old boy was something of a dandy and a ladies' man. Lots of neurotic, wealthy women patients. Let's see . . . he died in the flu epidemic of 1918. Tommy was the only child; he was overseas then. He came into the old boy's money the next year, when he was twenty-one. He got his discharge from the army over there and stayed in Paris and around Europe, spending his money. The doctor left him about $60,000, net, I believe, after the house in Washington Square had been sold and the debts paid off. Tommy got to know all the trans-Atlantic commuters and had a grand time—not throwing his money at the birds, but living the life of Riley. In 1925 he came back over here, practically

broke, and we canvassed the situation. In the old days he
would have become a wine agent and lived off his connections. He decided to turn professional gossip. He wanted
to start a weekly, but *Brevities* had just come a cropper and
The New Yorker was already going strong. Then he met Ted
Edwards, who had just bought the *Blade,* and they made
a deal."

"And he made a go of it," Maguire put in, encouragingly.

"He made a go of it because he had no fear, no faith
and no end of energy. He'd washed up all his illusions in
Europe. He wasn't a bookish man. He despised business
and the professions, except medicine, and he said a doctor
worked too hard and never made money unless he was a
genius or a quack. He became the Paul Pry of Manhattan,
but I never knew him to misuse his information for his
own profit."

"It's as honorable a calling as yours and mine, I suppose, Wylie," Maguire admitted. "Was Twitchell ever married?"

"No. I never knew a girl make him lose his head until
he met Miss Paris. And I think he showed excellent judgment there."

Maguire pondered.

"This case is going to be a hellion," he said. "How do
we know that the root of this murder don't go back to the
time he lived in Europe?"

"We don't," King admitted.

"And we don't know but what somebody he met on that
house party this week end might have followed him back
to town and shot him, do we?"

"No, but that seems unlikely."

"Man, the whole thing's unlikely. Here's Twitchell murdered in a theater lounge with a couple of thousand people
in the house. The average murder you can trace out along
a few lines and with the dirt the friends of the deceased'll

spill and what your stools bring in, you've got a chance to spot your killer. Most people have only a few friends and even fewer enemies. But this fellow had thousands of both and couldn't tell which most of 'em were, I'll bet."

He halted, went on: "This item about Marya Czerna's cooch dancing. If he'd broke off with her why did he keep on giving her publicity?"

King studied the column a moment.

"I connect that up with the item that precedes it," he said. "It's Tommy thumbing his nose at Czerna."

"What does that mean—French, ain't it?"

"An old Breton proverb," said King. *"Love is born of nothing and dies of everything.'"

"The French may be a funny race, but they sure know the facts of life," Rorty put in, grinning.

"Was he in love with Czerna?" Maguire pursued. "I mean, before he met this Miss—Patsy?"

"No, not in the romantic sense. The tie between them was physical, but it was very strong. I don't think even his falling in love with Patsy entirely destroyed that."

"You mean he was seeing her on the side?"

"No, I don't, Barney. Don't get me wrong. After Czerna found out he'd been rushing Patsy—and she found it out in less than a week—and she ordered Tommy to drop the girl, Tommy had her come up to his apartment the day after Thanksgiving—"

"Shane told us about that on the way over. She tried to knife him?"

"Yes. Well, Tommy wouldn't see her after that. I think possibly he was afraid to see her again—afraid, I mean, that she would get him back. She was the most voluptuous woman Tommy ever met, he told me, and he didn't spend seven years in Europe for nothing. He told me once that he was afraid if he lived with her too long he couldn't make the break."

"What was the matter with her, otherwise?"

"Well, Barney, you ought to know that these affairs of the flesh—well, it finally cloys. The girl is greedy, jealous, and as common as the back alleys of Bridgeport, where she grew up. She had only three things in her favor; she's gorgeous looking, she's voluptuous past all sanity and she was and perhaps still is mad about Tommy. But she wanted to be introduced to his friends, and while that was all right in a night club set, you understand how Tommy's old friends simply wouldn't receive her. She'd been harping on the matrimonial note, too. Tommy had been trying to get away from her for months before he met Patsy. I introduced them after the Harvard-Yale game at New Haven last fall and then I wished I hadn't, because Tommy fell in love for the first time since he grew up. And Patsy did too—and there she was all broiled up in this Czerna affair and Tommy's crazy life."

"You were interested in her yourself, Wylie?" Maguire asked, casually.

"I've been interested in her ever since she went into vaudeville when she was fourteen. Her aunt, who raised her, was a friend of mine."

"How old is the girl now?"

"Twenty-one last Christmas Eve."

"Well, let's get through this column before she comes and I'll talk to Czerna as soon as my brilliant skulls can find her."

"Does it seem likely to you she'd shoot him?" O'Neal spoke up. "Several people knew about her trying to stab him, you know."

"What people?"

"I was there, and so was Tommy's secretary, Preston, though he was in the back room. He came running in and helped me get the knife away from Marya. Then Tommy and I told Wylie about it, and Wylie went to see Marya and tried to talk her into a reasonable attitude."

"And what did she say?" Maguire inquired.

"She said she would give him until New Year's to get over this 'puppy love business with that little professional virgin' and come back to her. If he didn't, she was going to kill him and kill herself."

"Wasn't that just hot talk?" O'Neal demurred. "She loves life too much to kill herself, that girl!"

"I thought it was just bluff," said King, shaking his head. "Now I'm not sure."

"But why in hell should she have picked out that public place to kill him in?" O'Neal demanded, in exasperation.

"Why should *anybody* have picked it out, who wasn't crazy, drunk, coked up or desperate?" King countered. "That's why I think we'll find this shooting was done by an unbalanced person, and not planned in advance." He glanced at Maguire, who was studying the column.

"Women don't plan killings in advance, unless they're crazy," said the inspector, absently. "But that's the hottest trail we've picked up yet—this dame. Now what's this about the young publisher and the $70,000, I don't get it."

"That wasn't in Tommy's copy when I read it at two o'clock Friday morning," said O'Neal. "He means the fellow lost it in a crap game, Barney. He put it in later."

"Probably it didn't happen until after that," Rorty spoke up. "Them big crap games don't get going good until after midnight. But who's the sucker?"

"More than likely Ben Lincoln, of Lincoln and Lane," said King. "That's his weakness now."

"Him and plenty more," said Rorty, pityingly. "If a professional can't crack it, why should a Park Avenue amateur think he can? He'll have to sell a lot of books to stay with that gang."

"The Greeks had a word for it," said King, grimly. "Ego."

"Well, here's some Greek for you," Maguire cut in. "'John Gant and Claire Rivoli will consolidate as soon as the lawyers draw up the title guarantee.'"

"That's an item Tommy likely picked up on Long Island."

"When did he go out there?" Maguire asked.

"Sunday morning after the night joints closed," O'Neal answered. "Patsy was going to be rehearsing and resting all Sunday and Monday before the opening. He didn't get back until five o'clock Monday afternoon."

"How do you know?"

"Because he was to have dinner with me at the Colony at seven o'clock and I went by for him and he was just dressing. He said he had got back to town at five, had wasted a lot of time coming up in a taxi in traffic and had to stop to write something before he changed."

"He worked pretty hard?" Maguire prompted.

King answered him. "He took his job seriously. He particularly liked to scoop the news columns on engagements and sub rosa marriages, domestic scandals, and divorces among people who didn't want publicity. It was partly snobbery, I suppose, to show that he was on intimate terms with people who wouldn't talk to other newspaper men. Gant and Mrs. Rivoli are that sort."

"People of that sort don't shoot reporters, either," said Maguire. "But what does he mean by this?"

"It means that John Gant and Claire Rivoli are going to get married, and Tommy's gagging about the fact that they've each been married and divorced two and three times before," King explained. "I think that's right—this would be his third and her fourth."

"Companionate marriages, huh?" said Rorty. "Get up and change wives every so often, like the game we used to played with chairs."

"Marriage is like prohibition: only the poor respect it," said King, drily.

"More than likely you're right," said Maguire. "What's this crack about Rita Ahearn believing in Santa Klauss?"

"Rita is a show girl—or was. She's not so young any more and she doesn't get into the paper often. She probably phoned Tommy that item, herself, or had another girl send it in."

"Who gave her the pearl collar?"

"That German shipping man, Hans Klauss. He was over here before Christmas. Tommy might have added that he liked fat women; Rita's gained a lot of weight since she's been out of a job."

"You guys are the damnedest cynics," Maguire growled. "What's wrong with a nice plump woman? And Irish, at that."

"A cynic has been defined as one who judges all humanity by what he knows of himself," said King. "I like 'em lissom. And Rita Ahearn is a Polack, anyway."

"Well, you make me feel like a patsy, and I thought I knew my way about New York," Maguire growled.

It occurred to Nels that the inspector wasn't as dumb as he made himself out to be. He was playing on the vanity of Mr. King by assuming that the little man knew everything about Broadway and Park Avenue and the cross streets between. The Greeks had a word for that, all right. But Mr. King was pleasant, for all his cocksureness.

O'Neal had got to his feet and was striding about aimlessly, back of the grand piano and across the four tall windows that looked out over the black-and-mazda magic of Central Park. He stood now with his hands under the tails of his dress coat, staring out at the crazy quilt of upper Manhattan.

"Why doesn't that fellow get here with Pat—Miss Paris?" he demanded, turning and starting back.

"They'll be along," said Maguire, patiently. "Shall we go on with this, Shane?"

"By all means, Barney. Do you mind if I walk around? I'm not meself, tonight."

O'Neal was at the fireplace now, tugging at the back log with the tongs. Nels got up and took them from him, mended the fire, threw on another cedar log. Mr. O'Neal was evidently cold; Nels was so warm he wished he could shed his uniform coat.

"This item about Big Manny Murillo is just a gag," said King. "Though I don't know about the gangland merger part of it."

"That's a gag, too," said Maguire, sourly. "If them racketeers ever consolidated we could jail 'em under the anti-trust act, which is more than we can do under the criminal code."

"This item about Connie Crain surprises me," King spoke up, addressing O'Neal, who had resumed his pacing behind the divan. "I thought she was an Australian."

"She is," said O'Neal. "It says something about Birmingham, you mean? Well, couldn't it be Birmingham, England?"

King pondered it, before he spoke.

"All I know is that Saul Tabasco brought her over here under contract three years ago and announced her as an Australian actress. He likes to make a mystery of the private lives of his stars; it was Charles Frohman's idea and I still think it was better than this cheap publicity boloney we all put out on Broadway these days. Now here's Connie Crain, who won't have her pictures taken even for lobby displays. Look at the publicity she's got out of that freak affectation in just three years."

"Old Tabasco is the best press agent in the business and he will be when he's a hundred years old," O'Neal commented.

"That's interesting, gentlemen, but can't we be getting on," Maguire suggested. "I want to finish this before Miss Paris gets here. Is there anything in the item about the nude and the press agent?"

"Nothing but the truth. That's Frank Stayton and Merrill O'Malley." He spelled out the names for Rorty. "Stayton's neurotic and thinks Broadway gave him a dirty deal, but he wouldn't shoot Tommy for printing that."

"How about this Alice de Kosla?"

"Shane can answer that," said Wylie. "I barely know them."

"Her husband is Gerald Mudie, that English musical comedy tenor. Alice was his leading woman when he married her. She went abroad last Fall to do a picture in French and Hungarian, and when she came back he was living with a sculptress up in Westport. I hear she plowed out to that farmhouse in the snow last week with her lawyer, had an all-night conference, and went on to Reno next day."

"Now if she'd shot *him*—" Maguire mused. "Her husband, I mean—"

"Hell, she don't care *that* about him." O'Neal snapped his fingers. "She's been trying to get rid of him for a couple of years. She couldn't get a divorce in Paris because he wouldn't sign a waiver of appearance. Somebody must have cabled her to sneak back when she did."

"Is he still in love with her, do you suppose?" King wanted to know.

"They're both in love with themselves and faithful to themselves until death," O'Neal scoffed. "Everybody knows she's been living with Arthur for two years. Gerald's been hanging on to her because his voice is washed out and he may never get another good role either in musical comedy or in the pictures. Road companies, maybe, but he's through everywhere else. He had a grand voice until he was thirty, but he let it go to hell with booze and women."

"All right, then, the wife's in Reno. How about him and this sculptor woman?"

"They'd be too cockeyed to read this column, provided they saw it Monday, which they didn't. Cross them off."

"What's this about Manfred Wagenaar and the wives?" Maguire asked.

"The truth. He fell for this English girl, whose real name is Sneedon, not Morena, and married her because she was young and beautiful, after they had made a concert tour of the States. She was his accompanist. She was a disappointment to him as a wife and he's a practical Dutchman. He just went back to the first one in Holland. For a musician, he has rare good sense."

"He's out. Where's this second wife?"

"Living up at Carnegie Hall, trying to get concert bookings. Manfred's supporting her."

"Do you know her?"

"Well and unfavorably," said Shane.

"Would she shoot Twitchell for printing that?"

"Preposterous!" said Shane. "But—how should I know? She's the hysterical type."

"This item about Bruno the Basque wearing lavendar underwear was likely sent in by the Garden press agent," King volunteered.

"I don't know him," O'Neal said.

"Sure you do," said Sergeant Rorty. "Bruno Bolero the Toreador; the Basque Bruiser. He can't read English, and the sports writers kid the pants off him."

"I only see the championship bouts, Sergeant, I'm fed up with palookas."

"In this next one," said Maguire, "I suppose he means Maurice Alpert, the bootlegger. Who's Torres?"

"Lina Torres," Rorty supplied. "One of them chile queens in the movies. I saw her a lot with Alpert around his clubs, especially at the Del Oro before he sold it to Jack Jordan. She told me the talkies ruined her career."

"She was fired by the Hays office for being continually drunk and disorderly," King corrected him. "Her taking up with this Alpert here when she could have had the pick of Wall Street just about sizes her up. She'll never get anywhere because she has no judgment. She was thirsty when she got to New York, Alpert gave her a case of liquor, and she played around with him for a month, which is about her limit with one man."

"Should I call him and her in?" Maguire wondered.

"The item is a simple statement of fact. Why should either of them get sore?"

"All right. The next one I see with a name in it is this: 'Alberta Nash says she will never give him a divorce.'"

"It's a high fast one that only people who know their North Shore scandal will get," said King, grinning. "Tommy must have telephoned that in from Greenport. Tommy usually won't run an item on a married man cheating, but this one she evidently gave him. It's harmless."

"When Twitchell telephoned items, in that way, who takes 'em?" Maguire wanted to know.

"Any responsible person on the copy desk, I suppose," King hazarded. "I know Tommy always went to the *Blade* office just before they put his page to bed and read proof on it. It's too full of dynamite to risk anybody's blundering on it."

O'Neal, who was pacing up and down again, had picked up Rorty's clipping from the top of the grand piano.

"What former check-room girl is in the Social Register, Wylie?" he asked.

"I'll bite," said Wylie.

"Tommy was going to print the answer next week. He said most of the people in the Register wouldn't sleep at night until they found out. The answer was 'None.'"

Maguire chuckled.

The telephone buzzed, behind the tapestry. Rorty sprang up to answer it.

"It's for you, Inspector. I think it's Reed with Miss Paris, downstairs."

"Tell him to bring her up here," Maguire said.

"Now what have we got left to clean up in this column?" the inspector demanded, as O'Neal crossed the room and went out into the foyer. They heard him open the door into the elevator hallway. Wylie King got to his feet, too.

"We've got it all cleaned up," he said, folding the clipping and his sheet of notes and thrusting them into a pocket of his dressing gown. He crossed to the desk and replaced the blotter pad and the spare sheets of stationery. "Sufficient unto the day is the evil thereof. The rest of the column is just gags and oddities."

Sergeant Rorty got up from his seat alongside the piano, rubbing the cramp out of his writing hand.

"You said a mouthful that time, Mr. King," he exploded. "Ain't anybody on Broadway straight and decent?"

"You're going to meet one now," said King, looking toward the door.

They heard an elevator door roll open and shut. They heard footsteps on the tiled floor, a muffled exclamation. O'Neal's voice came roaring in from the hall:

"By God, you take that off her!"

A girl's voice, agonized:

"Don't, Shane! Don't! It's all right!"

The four men caromed through the foyer archway. Through the open hall door Nels, looking over Mr. King's head, could see a detective, his face beet red, fumbling with something brightly metallic on the wrist of a girl in a brown fur evening cape who was holding back Mr. O'Neal with one bare arm, and looking at him, pleadingly, over her left shoulder.

She turned her head just as the handcuff fell away from her wrist. The detective stepped back, uncertainly.

"Why in hell didn't you do as I told you?" Maguire rasped out. "This lady ain't no common criminal!"

"Inspector," said Reed, miserably, "I couldn't bring her no other way. When we got in the taxi she went crazy. We stop in traffic in Fifty-second Street and she jumps out of the cab and I chase her all the way back to the Del Oro. Three or four guys block me so she could get away. I got to the Del Oro, fin'ly, and there she is. She's run right into the arms of the officer on post in the doorway."

Nels studied the girl. She was all red-gold and ivory; a lovely figurine. Tears were trickling down her unrouged cheeks; the ivory was paling out now and she was swaying. Nels stepped around to catch her, but her two cavaliers had sprung to her support. Reed, unhappy and sullen, stood two paces behind her, Inspector Maguire in the doorway and Rorty behind him. Every eye was on the girl's white face; her eyes never left Maguire's.

The inspector broke the silence.

"Why, that's hard for me to believe," he said, gently cajoling. "What's the matter, child? What's come over you?"

She bit her lips.

"Why did you shoot at Jack Jordan?" he insisted, still gently, paternally.

Her voice burst out like a sob:

"I'll kill him! You can't stop me!" She tried to twist out of the grasp of her friends and all but succeeded.

"Why? Why do you want to kill him?" The inspector did not raise his voice from the murmur of incredulity and amazement.

She took a deep breath. Her head came up, her fine nostrils expanded like a thoroughbred's. Her voice flared out, metallic with suppressed hysteria:

"He killed Tommy! And I'm going to kill *him!*"

5

Patricia Paris, choking on the brandy O'Neal was holding to her lips, pushed him aside and sat up. She beckoned to the inspector, who was standing on the hearth rug with his back to the fire, watching her. The big man walked over to stand beside the divan, at her feet.

"Are you the head detective?" she whispered.

"This is Inspector Barney Maguire, in charge of the Homicide Squad," O'Neal told her. "Don't be afraid of him; he only wants to help you. I've known him since I was a lad."

"Do you feel like talking now?" Maguire asked, sympathetically.

Patsy cleared her throat.

"I want to talk," she said. She looked around at the six men standing about, apparently uncertain whether she should talk before them all.

"This is Sergeant Rorty, who is helping the Inspector," said Wylie King. "And this is Nels Lundberg, the fireman who found Tommy."

"Will you send that man away?" She looked across the room at the detective who had brought her over from the Del Oro Club.

Maguire waggled a thumb at the glowering Reed, indicating the foyer door. "Wait outside," his lips said, soundlessly. Reed withdrew. Maguire reassured her.

"He meant well, Miss Paris. He shouldn't have put the handcuffs on you, but you shouldn't have tried to run away from him. Where did you get that pistol?"

"Tommy gave it to me."

"When?"

"About a month ago."

"Why?"

"Because of Jack Jordan."

"What do you mean, child?"

She buried her face in her hands and began to shake anew with sobs. King and O'Neal, their faces stricken with misery, were sitting on either side of her now. Her fur cape had fallen back from her bare shoulders, the sweet sweep of her neck and throat emerged above an evening gown that looked as though it were made of beaten red gold.

The blond Norwegian lad in the blue uniform found himself plotting crazily to pick up this girl, fight off these detectives and take her away from there. Thirty-three stories above the street in the penthouse of the Park Tower—it was too much to expect of Douglas Fairbanks, himself, and Nels had no sword. He had to smile at the thought of fighting his way backward down thirty-two flights of stairs with a rapier in one hand and a helpless girl over the other arm. He couldn't do a thing but keep quiet, or they'd send him away.

The little dancer was stifling the last of her sobs, now. She dabbed at her eyes with a wisp of lace; Nels stepped forward and handed her a clean handkerchief. She took it without looking at him, used it.

"I'm all right now," she said, gasping for breath. "I'll try not to do that again."

"That's the girl," said Maguire, cheeringly. He reached behind him and hauled a chair over near the divan. "Let's all sit down," he said. Rorty and Nels sat down together on the piano bench, facing the divan.

"Now tell me about Jordan," the inspector suggested. "Do you mind if I smoke?" Apparently he wanted to put the girl at her ease.

"Please do," she said, with a small smile. "Wylie, have you a cigarette for me?"

Wylie lighted one for her. After a few deep puffs, she began talking, in a low, fairly calm voice.

"I don't know what started Jordan annoying me, but about a month ago he began. He would be waiting at the stage door when I came out of rehearsals—someone must have been keeping him posted on when I'd be out; because his car would be parked in the back street and he'd offer to take me home or wherever I was going. I'd never met the man, but he seemed to think it was enough just to tell me who he was, as though he were the Prince of Wales. I would never go with him, though I was always polite to him. I've always been afraid of gangsters. I've worked hard since I was ten years old to be a dancer. If you want to be a great dancer you have to practice like Paderewski. You don't go to night clubs, or at least I never did until I met Tommy." Her voice caught in her throat. "And I had never been in Jordan's club, ever."

"You and Mr. Twitchell were in love?" Maguire hinted.

"We were going to be married." She bit her lip, looked down at the square emerald on her ring finger, fought for control.

"When did he give you the ring?" Maguire asked.

"A month ago. But I wouldn't wear it until *Rebel Rose* opened. This is my first Broadway production, and I wanted to see what sort of notices I'd get. If the critics knew I was engaged to Tommy some of them might be kinder to me. I wore it for luck tonight. We were going to announce the engagement, or maybe just go and get married, this week."

"Where does your family live, Miss Paris?"

"My parents both died before I was four years old."

King explained, "They were in show business; they had what we call a rep company. They were very well known through the Middle West. Patricia was brought up by her aunt, the great Petra Paris, the dancer."

Maguire beamed. "I saw her at Madison Square Garden when I was a lad," he said, warmly. "She did a fire dance with long scarfs—yards of them. Well, well,—do you still live with her?"

Patsy shook her head.

"Petra Paris died last year, Barney," O'Neal answered for her. "If she had lived until last night she'd have seen her life work crowned with a great triumph. This child got an ovation after her last dance that I've never seen the like of for a dancer in a musical production."

"I'm glad to hear it. I'm sorry I missed it, Miss Paris. Now tell me why you think Jordan—did this."

Patsy swallowed, began slowly.

"When I went back to my dressing room after the first act finale, he was sitting there, waiting for me. He had a regular hat box full of orchids."

"How did he get in?" King asked, frowning.

"That's the first thing I asked him, and he said: 'Don't you know who I am, baby? I'd like to see the guy that would tell me I couldn't get in anywheres.' I laughed at him. I said: 'Well, here's the guy that's going to tell you to get out. I've got to dress for the second act.'" She halted, breathed deeply, went on:

"He said all he wanted was to invite me on a little party after the show; I could bring one of my girl friends. He wanted to give a little supper for me up at the Del Oro. Well, I didn't want to go anywhere with him, ever, and I particularly didn't want to go to the Del Oro, because that Czerna girl runs the show and wisecracks about the guests." She hesitated.

"I know all about Miss Czerna," said Maguire, helpfully.

Patsy nodded. "He told me, the first time he talked to me, that he had just bought the Del Oro, just as another kind of social climber might say: 'Well, I'm in Newport society now. I bought a house there.'"

"To get back to last night, Miss Paris—"

"Well, I told him I was going to Mr. Edwards' party. 'With who?' he said. I was angry, and I blurted out: 'With Mr. Twitchell and Shane O'Neal.' He just grinned with those horrible decayed teeth and said: 'O'Neal don't count and I can fix it with your boy friend.' I said how could he fix it and he said: 'Oh, he'll be nice. He knows me.' I said he was insulting not only me but Mr. Twitchell with a statement like that—I was so furious I can't remember just what I said. He said: 'He'll be nice. I'll tell him you're going with me.' He started to get up and his derby hat fell on the floor and he leaned over to pick it up and his shirt front buckled and—" she swallowed—"I saw the pistol. It was here." She indicated the curve of her left armpit. "That's where Tommy carries his, so I knew right away what it was."

"Wait," said Maguire. "You say Twitchell carried a pistol?"

"He had a permit to do it. He only carried it when he was going around really tough places. He never had it on when he went out with me; I made him promise not to; I thought he was safer without it, because, even though he had practiced until he was a very good shot, I didn't think he'd have a chance against a real gunman."

"That was one of Tommy's idiosyncrasies, Barney," Wylie King put in. "I told him he was foolish to carry a gun, but it fulfilled some small boy wish of his. One thing, at least—he never let anyone know he carried it."

King shook his head negatively.

"Not even when he was drinking?"

"He didn't drink. Not since he went on the *Blade*,—except a drink or two among friends, off duty—if he was ever off duty. He would take a highball or two with Shane and me if we were up when he got home in the morning. He never drank in night clubs nor at cocktail parties and he took mineral water in speakeasies."

"Was he afraid of being killed?" Rorty spoke up.

"Not half so much as his friends were afraid for him. He was a fatalist—if he got it, he got it."

The tears were rolling down the girl's cheeks again.

"He didn't have a gun on tonight, I know," said O'Neal. "He was late getting dressed and I was in his place—" he indicated the adjoining penthouse by a move of his head and eyes—"while he was tying his tie and putting on his coat."

"He didn't have either a rod or a holster on when we found him," Rorty supplied.

"Now to get back to Jordan, Miss Paris," Maguire pursued. "Did he leave you after he bragged about Mr. Twitchell's being nice to him?"

"He didn't leave me until the stage manager came around checking up five minutes before the second act curtain. I wasn't dressed at all when the stage manager stuck his head into the dressing room, and he started giving me what I deserved for holding the show up. Jordan gave him a dirty look, but he didn't know Jordan and he just blistered me."

"Why weren't you ready—because Jordan was there?" Maguire asked.

Miss Paris nodded. A blush spread over her throat and face.

"I didn't know what to do. I was afraid Tommy would hit him and he would hit Tommy with the pistol or maybe shoot if he found him out front. So I just held him in my dressing room until Tommy had time to get back to his seat for the second act. I had to think in a hurry, but I decided to do that and then to send a note to Tommy asking him to come backstage after my dance in second act

opening. I was sure I could persuade Tommy to stay out of
Jordan's way. Then I was going to dress after my last dance
and go out through the auditorium and meet Tommy. That
would have meant not appearing in the finale, but I knew
I could explain to Mr. Wilde, somehow. All I had to do in
the finale was walk on, anyway."

"Where was your dresser all this time?" King asked,
frowning.

"She wasn't there. I called out in the corridor for her—
her name's Rosie, and Jordan said: 'You want your maid? I
sent her out for a package of cigarettes.' He had given her
twenty dollars and told her to keep the change, but she
went because he scared her out of her wits. She's always
talking about gangsters, and Jordan told her who he was
and she didn't come back until she was sure he was gone."

"How do you know all that, Miss Paris?"

"Rosie told me. As soon as Jordan left she came in,
so weak in the knees that she could hardly stand up. She
broke down and almost had hysterics and begged me not
to discharge her; she couldn't get another job. I told her
to brace up and shut up and forget it, but her hands shook
so that she took an agonizing time to hook me into that
tiny costume. I made her keep the twenty dollars and told
her to go home, that I'd dress myself for the finale. But
I put on these clothes instead and went out through the
auditorium. Tommy hadn't come backstage as I told him
to. He wasn't in his seat, though Shane was. I didn't dare
go down and talk to Shane for fear Jordan would see me.
I asked the doorman if Tommy had gone out, and he said
no, at least he hadn't seen him. The only place I could
think of was the lounge downstairs, but just as I started
down there, I saw Mr. Flaxon running up the stairs and I
dodged into the shadow because I didn't want him to see
me cutting the finale. So I went out through the lobby and
walked over to Broadway and got a taxi and went home."

"Where do you live, Miss Paris?"

"I live in Topless Towers."

Maguire's face showed that he didn't know the place.

"That's the new studio apartment house on the other side of the street in this same block, down towards Sixth Avenue," King explained.

"Why did you go home?" Maguire wanted to know, still casually.

"I just gave the driver the address automatically when I got into the cab. For one thing, I wanted to telephone to Tommy's apartment and make sure he was safe."

"You expected him to go there?"

"Yes, he always goes home after a show and writes up what he has picked up during the evening, for next day's paper."

"The arrangement was," O'Neal spoke up, "that Miss Paris should meet us at Edwards'. I had volunteered to call for her but she said it would save trouble just to meet at Ted's."

"Did you call Mr. Twitchell when you got home?" Maguire asked.

"Three times, about every ten minutes. He didn't answer. I supposed Preston was out. I was still worried about Tommy, but there wasn't anything I could do about it until I found him."

"What time did you leave home?"

"About a quarter to one."

"Where did you go then?"

"I walked over to Mr. Edwards'. It's only about four blocks, and I felt so upset I didn't want to get in a cab. Just riding over from the theatre in one had made me sort of seasick. I took some bicarbonate when I got to my apartment, but—it came up."

"Emotionally upset," said King.

Maguire prompted: "Then what?"

She fought for control again. "He took me into his bedroom as soon as I got there and told me Tommy had been hurt. I knew—right then—I could see it in his eyes—that Tommy was dead." Her voice failed.

"Edwards went out to tell his guests that he was called away by an emergency at the paper," King supplied, "and when he came back for her she was gone."

"What did you do then, child?" Maguire inquired, gently.

"I went over to the Del Oro Club to find Jordan."

"In a taxi?"

"No. I walked. The traffic on this street goes east and I wanted to go west, and—well, I was just beside myself and I didn't want to get into a traffic jam and have to sit there, doing nothing."

"What did you intend to do?"

"I don't honestly know. I don't think I got the idea of killing that man until I saw him and all of a sudden when he grinned at me with those dirty teeth of his and said: 'So you came over, after all, didn't you, baby?'—that was exactly what he said, Inspector.—I just opened my bag without taking my eyes off his face and got the pistol and let off the safety catch with my thumb and pulled the trigger and the pistol jumped clear out of my hand. . . ." She closed her eyes, swallowed.

"Go on," Maguire prompted.

"He put his hand up to his shoulder—he was still looking at me, but he wasn't grinning any more. I thought he was reaching for his pistol and I lost my head and ran out through the door and down the stairs."

"What stairs?"

"Jordan's office in the Del Oro is on a little balcony up a flight of circular stairs," King explained. "He was in the office when you shot at him, wasn't he, Patsy?"

"Yes," she said, leaning her head back wearily against the divan's top. "If I didn't kill him, when you let me go I'm going to kill him. I don't care how long you keep me in jail, I'll kill him when I get out." Her voice was monotonous; Nels could see a pulse beating in the blue veined ivory of her throat.

"Somebody else will attend to that, child," said Maguire, soothingly. "If he killed Tommy Twitchell he'll burn for it, and burn quick. You take my word for that. Now tell me, Miss Paris, did you have your pistol with you at the theatre tonight?"

She shook her head negatively, without opening her eyes.

"It was at home. I got it when I went home."

Maguire's voice was suddenly sharp: "You really went home to get that pistol, didn't you, Miss Paris?"

She shook her head, wearily.

"I told you, Inspector, that I wasn't planning what to do. I just did it. I didn't know then that Tommy . . ."

"Then why did you put the pistol in your handbag?"

"I was afraid—of what Jordan might do if Tommy should start a fight with him."

"You wanted to protect Mr. Twitchell and you were afraid of Jordan so you took the pistol with you. But you were going to Mr. Edwards', weren't you? You didn't expect Jordan to be there?"

"Mr. Maguire, please don't ask me again why I took the pistol. I've told you all I know about why I took it. I had a feeling that something terrible was going to happen."

Maguire's voice softened. "Now tell us what happened after you shot Jordan and ran down the stairs."

"I bumped smack into this man—this detective who brought me over here. He grabbed me."

"Did he know you had shot Jordan?"

"How could he? Jordan was upstairs."

"Then what happened?"

"This detective took me back upstairs. I fought him all the way up."

"What did Jordan say?"

"He wasn't there."

"So? Where was he?"

"I don't know. There were just a couple of waiters and a big man who seemed to be the manager or something."

"Who told Reed—the detective—that you had shot Jordan?"

"The manager. He was cursing at me." She shuddered.

"Didn't he say anything about where Jordan was?"

"He said Jordan had gone to a doctor."

"That couldn't have been more than two or three minutes after you fired the shots."

She considered. "Not more than two minutes."

"Did Jordan come down the stairway after you going out?"

Patricia paused for thought. "He couldn't have, because I bumped into the detective at the bottom of the stairs—they're very narrow and spiral so you can't pass anyone on them. And the detective took me right upstairs and Jordan wasn't there."

"Another way out," Maguire concluded. "Did you notice another door?"

Patricia thought. "Yes," she said, still not opening her eyes. "There was a narrow door in the paneling at the back wall. Jordan was standing against it, at the side of the desk. You haven't found him yet, have you?"

"It hasn't been reported to me if they have," said Maguire. "Now why did you jump out of the cab and run all the way back to the Del Oro?"

Patricia opened her eyes, raised her head, looked at the inspector in astonishment.

"To kill him. I didn't think I had, the first time."

"Where was the pistol then—in your bag?"

"No. I must have dropped it. I think it kicked right out of my hand."

"You're lucky you didn't shoot yourself," Maguire shook his head, sadly. "You must have been out of your mind, girl, running back to that place to kill a man when you had lost your gun."

"I didn't realize I didn't have the gun. Anyway, I'd have killed him with a chair or something. I'm pretty strong."

"You're certainly strong-willed," the inspector chuckled. "You would have been doing the New York Police Department and the people of New York a great service if you had killed that weasel. But don't be telling your lawyer I said that, or I'll have to make a liar out of you."

"I won't, Inspector. Will they put me in jail?"

"Don't you bother about that," O'Neal spoke up. "Wylie and I will tend to that."

"You mean you'll go my bail?" She smiled, weakly. "Well, I won't run away. All I want to do is stay here and see Jack Jordan get his."

Maguire demurred: "You don't really know that Jordan killed Twitchell, Miss Paris? I mean you have no evidence except the conversation you had in your dressing room?"

Patsy pondered. "I guess that's all," she said. "But isn't that enough?"

"I'm afraid it isn't enough to convict him, unless we can get a lot more on him."

"One point, Inspector," Sergeant Rorty spoke up. "Jordan must have been in her dressing room at least twenty minutes. What did they talk about all that time? What she's told us they said wouldn't have taken up more than five minutes."

The girl was blushing again, a wave of pink flooding up through the transparent velvet of her skin from the red gold decolletage to the roots of the red gold hair coiled in a heavy rope around the crown of her little head.

"I was just killing time. I had to hold him there until Tommy got back to his seat. I vamped him. He must have stayed fifteen minutes after he first started to go, but it seemed like an hour."

"What do you mean—vamped him?" Maguire asked.

"Well, he was starting off to find Tommy and I said why did he have to rush off, so I began taking off my costume, and he stayed." Her tone was so naively triumphant that every man in the room had to smile. It didn't seem possible to Nels that she could blush any more intensely, but she did.

"I did some perfectly terrible things," she went on, miserably. "I changed behind the screen, but I came out with just a robe on and made him powder my back, and all the time I was laughing and talking perfect nonsense. Then he pulled me over on his lap and tried to kiss me." She shuddered. "I was too strong for him—he really isn't strong at all."

"He's a snowbird," Rorty corroborated.

She looked at him questioningly. "You mean he takes drugs?"

Rorty nodded.

"Then he must have been coked up tonight," she said. "I was sure he was drunk, but there wasn't any liquor on his breath."

"He never takes a drink," said Rorty. "Go ahead."

"Well, I was sitting on his lap and listening to his bragging about what a swell dame he'd make of me, when the stage manager poked his head in the door. That's what made Paul lose his temper; me sitting on a man's lap—and a man like that—instead of being dressed. He bawled us both out, terribly."

"Didn't Jordan tell him who he was?" King asked.

"He didn't open his mouth. He just gave Paul a dirty look. Paul finally said: 'Get out of here. Can't you understand plain English?' And Jordan mumbled to me he was sorry and slunk out. He left his hat on the makeup shelf but he didn't come back for it."

"What was this about the note?" Maguire asked.

"Before I went on for the second act opening ballet I wrote a note to Tommy and sent it out to his seat. Rosie took it out and gave it to an usher to give to him."

"Did he get it, or do you know?"

"I don't know. Rosie said he did, but I had no time to check up. All I know is that he didn't come backstage as I told him to. That's what started me really worrying about him."

It was Shane O'Neal who was embarrassed and red-faced now. "Wait a minute, Barney," he said. "I give you my word I forgot all about this." He fished a folded bit of powder blue paper out of his pocket, leaned over and handed it to Maguire. The inspector unfolded it, studied it. He looked up.

"It just says: 'Come back stage at once and find me. Imperative.' It's not signed."

"I didn't want to sign it, in case it went astray. Tommy knew my writing."

"I knew her writing, too," said O'Neal, "just by looking at 'Mr. Twitchell—Rush' on the outside. I got up and went to the back of the house looking for Tommy, but I couldn't find him, so I stuck the note in my pocket. I thought it was just a sweet message for him. Naturally, I didn't read it."

"What time was that, about?" Maguire quizzed.

O'Neal pondered, staring into the fire. "Just before the curtain went up—the second act curtain. You remember, I spoke to you, Wylie, and asked you if you'd seen Tommy."

"That's right. And I introduced you to Perry Hamilton."

"You had no premonition, then, that anything had happened to him?" Maguire pursued, watching O'Neal narrowly.

"Nothing could have been farther from my mind. My mind was backstage, with this child."

Patricia covered his right hand with her left one, on which the big emerald winked its green eye.

"One thing more, Miss Paris," Maguire began, and hesitated. "Were you living with Mr. Twitchell—as man and wife would live together, I mean?"

King and O'Neal started up, said the same words: "Don't answer that."

"Barney," said King, after a moment of tense silence. "This girl has no legal counsel. I know you're—"

"The question was official, not personal, Miss Paris," Barney growled, reddening. "I withdraw it. You will be asked that later, probably, when you make a formal statement of what you know about this case." He paused, modified his tone. "You are so far accused of no crime, except that we shall have to make a complaint against you for violation of the Sullivan Act in possessing a pistol without a permit, and carrying a concealed weapon and, if Jordan can be found and will produce any witnesses or make the complaint, you may be indicted for assault with intent to kill. Resisting an officer—"

O'Neal and King were both on their feet now. So was Nels, across the room. King held the big Irishman in check with his left arm.

"Barney, is it really necessary that you should be brutal to this girl?" he demanded. His tone was calm but icy.

"I merely wished to remind her," said the inspector, "that she is in jeopardy and the best way she can help herself out of it is to tell the truth, the whole truth and nothing but the truth, or even you two can't help her."

"But, Inspector," Patsy spoke up, astonished and indignant. "I wasn't violating the law carrying a pistol! I have a permit! Tommy got me the permit before he gave me the pistol."

"Good God!" said Maguire. His tone conveyed that he washed his hands of all New York officialdom.

"He taught me to shoot it, he told me never to pull it unless I had to, and then to shoot at a man's stomach and shoot to kill. He got me a heavy automatic—not the heaviest, but a thirty-eight. He said there was no use in a woman's carrying a pistol unless it would knock a man down with the first shot."

"A night club cowboy," said Rorty, grimly, under his breath to Nels on the bench beside him.

"If it was a thirty-eight and you hit your man square, you may get your wish yet," said Maguire darkly. His tone mollified. "Well, Shane, you and Mr. King and you, little lady, I want you all to forget that we had any sharp words just now. We are still just six representatives of the people of New York, three of us close friends of Mr. Twitchell, all trying our best to get some clue to who killed him. Is that understood?"

He looked from one to the other of the three.

"Thank you, Barney, it is," said King. The tension relaxed.

"Now I propose to go into Twitchell's apartment," said the inspector, rising. "I suggest that Miss Paris spare herself that. Perhaps she could lie down on one of your beds, Shane. If we need her we'll send for her."

Patsy looked from O'Neal to King and back to O'Neal.

"That seems to me both wise and kind," the host said. King nodded.

"Get her comfortable, Shane, and then join us. Now, little lady, I'm going to send Mr. Reed back in here to take any telephone calls for me that come in on this wire. He won't bother you, but if you want anything you can call him and he'll call one of us."

Patsy nodded assent.

"Shane, have you got a key to Twitchell's place, did you say?"

"Wylie, will you take care of Pat?" said the host. "I've got a key on my chain here. We'll have to go around by the terrace. I'll be right back."

King rejoined the inspector and the fireman presently in the living room of Tommy Twitchell's part of the penthouse. Rorty had gone downstairs on some errand for the inspector. O'Neal had returned to his own apartment.

Twitchell's apartment was wholly in the modernistic mode, from the silver and black of the walls to the chrome-nickel-iron alloy frames and trim of the furniture. Across the blank partition wall opposite the entrance was the largest divan Nels had ever seen: semi-circular, covered with heavy material in stripes of black and silver radiating out from the wall like the ribs of a fan. A person could lie full length—yes, ten people could lie on it with their heads together near the wall and their feet out like the spokes of a wheel. All the chairs were low, with huge square cushions and bright metal tubing frames. Nels sat down in one; it was surprisingly comfortable. Even the heavy, velvety rug was black and silver in a crazy chain lightning pattern. Not a restful room, but certainly a striking one, Nels concluded; it must have cost a mint of money.

Nels sat back in the left-hand corner of the room, which was not as large as the O'Neal living room, but still at least twenty-five feet square. The wall at his left divided this room from O'Neal's adjoining apartment. The wall facing him contained the flat archway opening into the foyer which gave onto the elevator hall. To the left in the foyer there was a door which must, Nels judged, open into an inside fire stairway. To the right of the foyer arch in the living room wall was another flat archway leading into a small room, about twelve feet square, which had been Mr. Twitchell's office. It was all modernistic, too, in bright metal trim and black paneling and furniture to match. Nels could see in the glass of a French door that led onto the roof terrace the reflections of a desk, a typewriter stand of a special design, a bank of filing cabinets, all in black and silvery metal, and a Dictaphone. Mr. Twitchell was evidently methodical.

Seeing the Dictaphone excited Nels. In the last mystery story he had read a Dictaphone record had given the clue that had trapped the murderer. He itched to get at this one. Two things held him back: he didn't know how to operate a Dictaphone, and he didn't want to attract too much of Inspector Maguire's attention lest he be sent back to the fire station and miss the excitement. Moreover, he didn't want to go off and leave Miss Paris. He recognized that she didn't know he was on earth and probably never would, but he had joined the company of the brawny Mr. O'Neal and the learned Mr. King as one of her three mus-keteers. She was the first girl he had ever encountered who seemed lovely and tragic enough to be a proper Milady out of the Dumas stories, which he had read in Norwegian, back in the old country as a boy.

Mr. King was talking to the inspector in the office, while Maguire opened and shut drawers, evidently just exploring.

"I didn't want to upset Patsy again," Mr. King's voice came around the corner, "but I've got something to add about Jordan. When I came out of the theatre tonight, I was almost run over by a car. Jack Jordan was in it."

"You're sure?" the inspector demanded.

"His isn't a face you'd mistake for anyone's else in New York, with that claret stain on the right cheek that looks like a map of South America."

"It does, at that," Maguire agreed.

"The Wilde show had bored me, and I was going across the street to catch the last of Sue Starling's show—it was opening at the Nichols, you know. I stopped to pat the horse of the mounted cop in front of the New Netherland and then I walked out into the street and almost got hit by this black sedan. Jordan was in the car, sitting by the chauffeur. I jumped back and his face wasn't two feet from mine when the car went past my knees, with the brakes full on. They went on more slowly and turned the corner of Seventh Avenue, to the right, going downtown. I wondered where Jordan was going without his hat and overcoat. I went on over to the Nichols and came home after that show was out. The Wilde show wasn't out—that was about five after twelve."

Nels could see Maguire sitting on the edge of the broad desk, reflected in the glass of the French door, pondering.

"Maybe it wasn't much of a mystery, Wylie," he said, finally. "He said he would wait for Miss Paris at the stage door. He had his car parked facing east, maybe, on Forty-second Street, over west of Eighth Avenue, say. The street behind the theatre is a one-way, west bound. Wasn't it natural that he should go out and have the car driven around behind the theatre, and go along so he would know where the driver parked it?"

"Absolutely logical," said King. "If I had heard Patsy's story before, I might have figured it out, myself."

A telephone bell whirred. Nels jumped. It was the telephone on Mr. Twitchell's desk in there. Mr. King was answering it.

Mr. King talked so low at first that Nels couldn't hear half he said. He seemed to be telling someone that someone was not here, but that he was waiting for him, too. Nels strained to hear.

"Why don't you come up and wait for him?" Mr. King was saying. A pause. "All right, if you want to talk to him alone, I'll beat it. . . . Well, if it's that important, come on up. Listen, are you downstairs now? . . . Oh, I see." He was talking louder, now "Wait a minute; the other phone is ringing. Hold the wire." Mr. King whispered to the inspector; he resumed talking. "Where are you now? Fifty-fifth and Sixth? In the drugstore? Well, why don't you walk on over here? Will you? . . . Atta girl!"

King replaced the telephone with a clatter. "Where's Rorty?" he shot at the inspector. "Downstairs talking to the telephone operators and the doormen. Checking up."

"Can I take him? I want to head her off and bring her up the service elevator to dodge the reporters. They'll be after her like wolfhounds—they know she's connected with both Twitchell and Jordan." King was out in the foyer, now, opening the door to the hall. "I want to get her up here before we spring it on her that Tommy's been killed."

"Hell, she knows that! She let on to Reed that she didn't, but you know she must. It's all over Broadway by now."

"If she knew it when she was talking to me, Barney, she's a better actress than I ever thought she was."

"Well, what was on her mind, then?"

"I shouldn't be surprised if it weren't the same thing that was on Patsy's mind," said King, slowly. "When I answered the phone, she thought I was Tommy's confidential man, Preston, and she said 'Is Tommy there?' I told her no, and who I was, and she said: 'Well, listen, get hold of him and tell him I said to stay away from the Del Oro and Jack Jordan, whatever he does, until he sees me.' Then I got her to promise to come on over here. I don't want the reporters to get at her."

"Sure. I'll go downstairs with you," said Maguire.

The buzzer over their heads whirred angrily, two, three, four times. Even the inspector started at the sound. King opened the door, cautiously. Nels had got to his feet, out of the soft pillows of the deep chair. But it was only Detective Reed, to say that headquarters wanted Inspector Maguire on the private line in O'Neal's apartment.

"Bring Czerna up here," Maguire said, following King out. "Don't tell her until I get here. If she's acting, I'll bet I can tell it." The door closed.

Left alone in the dead man's apartment, Nels made straight for the Dictaphone. He punched buttons, moved gadgets on the machine until, guided by the word "Repeat" he discovered how to make the record play back what was recorded on it.

He heard Mr. Twitchell, in a pleasant, sharp voice, instructing his stenographer about a letter to the president of a woman's club in Montclair, New Jersey, who wanted him to talk on the Place of Publicity in Building Civic Consciousness. "You know, Miss Sullivan, tell her no and make her like it. Not high hat—something she can hand down to her grandchildren." Evidently Mr. Twitchell had a sense of humor about himself.

Nels played back the nearly used up cylinder three times, trying to find something that a detective story writer could make a clue of, but it just wasn't there. He listened with one guilty ear alert for any noise at the front door, but finally gave up the Dictaphone. He wandered unhappily toward the back of the house; he poked his head into Mr. Twitchell's bedroom. On a low modern dresser of inlaid brown wood a large and exquisite photograph of Miss Patricia Paris stood in a silver easel frame. The wide clear eyes seemed to be looking straight at Nels. He backed out of the room. In the corridor again, he smelled something—something burning or burnt. He went prowling through to the rear of the apartment, opening doors to inspect a guest bedroom with its own bath, a dining room, a small but elaborate kitchen and pantry, various closets, and finally, up a short corridor, a small bedroom.

The odor was coming from this room. It smelled like a smoldering hair mattress. Nels stepped into the room, and stopped in his tracks.

The distant whir of a buzzer disturbed his careful survey of that small room. The buzzer was going continuously, angrily, as he hurried back through the corridor to the front of the apartment. He opened the door into the elevator hall, expecting to see Maguire or King. He confronted both of them, along with Sergeant Rorty and a tall, opulently curved, defiant beauty in a brown fur coat that must be sable. Her face was startling with stage makeup and there was a circlet of rhinestones across her wealth of silver blonde hair. Her eyes were a deep chestnut brown, and very large—Mr. O'Neal had said Marya Czerna was a blonde Italian. Nels had time to inspect her, because the three men were looking at her with their backs to the door Nels had opened. Maguire turned.

"Here's the fire department," he said. "The house could have burned down while you were answering that bell, boy!" He laughed, mirthlessly, but Nels did not even smile.

"I was in the back of the house," he said in his carefully chosen English. "I thought I smelled something burning." His voice was playing tricks with him, and he had to step back as they filed past him, into the living room. Nels, following, starting to speak, saw Inspector Maguire whirl on Marya Czerna, like a cat upon a mouse.

"Who killed Tommy Twitchell?" he snapped.

The blonde Madonna of the night clubs looked at him, frowning. Gradually the words seemed to penetrate her understanding. She put one be-diamonded hand up to her throat.

"Who *killed Tommy?*" she repeated, unbelieving.

"He's dead. Shot. At the theatre. Don't tell me you didn't know that." There was almost a sneer in Maguire's measured tones.

There was no answer. The lady had relaxed, rather than fallen, over onto the semi-circular divan. Her sable coat, the blue-white voluptuousness of her bosom above the calyx of a startlingly blue evening gown, her tapered legs in blue silk and her slim feet in blue slippers, the brown satin lining of her coat, and her mop of white gold hair all made a bizarre pattern on the black and silver ribs of the couch cover. She looked like a lady painted on a giant fan. They all stood staring at her.

"Get some water, will you, boy," Maguire snapped, vexed at these collapsible females.

The fireman started obediently for the kitchen. In the corridor doorway he turned. He spoke, as usual, deliberately, but this time with a mild exasperation:

"Inspector," he said. "I tried to tell you before: there's another dead man back there."

6

Nels opened the door at the end of the short corridor. The air within was foul with fumes; stale smoke dimmed the light from a ceiling panel of ground glass and a prismatic reading lamp on a table beside the bed. At the left of the door stood a tall chest of drawers topped by a wall mirror. Beyond it along the left-hand wall, with its head next the single window opposite the door, was a three-quarter width bed. Next to the window, in the right-hand wall, a mirrored door, partly open, led into a bathroom tiled in black and white. The bed and the chest were in brown wood inlaid with silvery metal alloy; the two chairs were of bent tubing of the same metal with brown leather seats and backs. A rug in black and silver covered most of the floor, about ten by twelve feet; the bedspread was black and silver in a crazy block pattern; the walls were silvered, with black stripes.

Nels was looking at the furnishings; the three other men had eyes only for what was alongside the bed.

"Preston!" King called out sharply.

Inspector Maguire strode across the rug and dropped to his knees beside the figure in the tweed suit lying across an open steamer trunk whose lid rested against the edge of the mattress. The man's head was on the bed, face turned to the right and away from the observers, his left cheek on the counterpane. His body sagged in an unnatural curve across the open trunk, the back uppermost, the weight resting on the head and the knees; the lower legs extending almost straight out behind so that the dark brown oxfords nearly touched the partition wall next to the bathroom door. He was a tall man, slender but well built.

Maguire touched the right cheek with the back of his hand, held it there, looked over his shoulder.

"He's cold," he announced.

King walked over to peer down at the body; Sergeant Rorty and the fireman leaned across the end of the bed.

"Twitchell's valet?" Rorty asked.

"No. His confidential man. He had no valet; only a maid from the building service."

"Shot in the back of the head." The inspector's big forefinger indicated the spot, just above the nape of the neck in the curly brown hair. "Get me a towel," he said to the fireman. Nels brought a face towel from the bathroom rack. The inspector covered his left hand with it and raised the man's head off the counterpane. All four peered under it.

"That's where the smudge came from," said Rorty. "Funny that a bullet should set the bed afire."

Maguire pointed down at the lid of the steamer trunk.

"Cigar ashes. He was smoking when he was shot; that's what set the bed afire. Here's the wet end of the cigar."

They studied the burned patch, as large as the palm of a man's hand. The blanket under the counterpane was burned through and the mattress charred.

"He must have fallen face down, with the cigar in his mouth."

Maguire had rolled the head around; now he replaced it carefully in the original position, wiped his hands on the towel.

It was a handsome face, with an aquiline nose, a long chin and a high forehead, of a type that the movies had taught Nels to recognize as that of an English gentleman. The inspector's next words confirmed the fireman's judgment.

"This fellow don't look like a servant," he said to King.

"He wasn't," King said. "There's no doubt he was well born and educated. Englishman, of course. But he'd never talk about his past."

"He's dressed like a gentleman," said Rorty, whose own tweeds and linen were beyond criticism.

"Tommy paid him liberally."

"Twitchell must have thought a lot of him, eh?" Maguire asked.

"He did. He'd had him less than a year, but he hoped to keep him until one of them died of old age. He was always afraid, though, that the fellow would turn out to be the Earl of Something and leave him flat."

"He'll never be the earl of anything now," said Maguire.

"Rigor mortis set in?" King asked.

"Just beginning, I'd say. He's not stone cold yet."

"How long has he been dead?"

"Something between two and four hours, I'd guess." Maguire got ponderously to his feet and took out his thin gold watch from his waistcoat. "It's 2:29 now; you must have come in here about 2:20 a.m." He was addressing Nels. "You didn't disturb anything?"

"The only thing I did was to turn on the lights at the switch by the door there. You were ringing the buzzer at the front door. I went over and touched his cheek like you did, Inspector, and then I went up front and let you in."

"Funny we didn't smell this smudge before," Maguire said.

"This place is fireproof," said Nels. "The door's tight. You could burn up everything in this room and it wouldn't spread if that metal door was closed. I didn't smell anything until I got to the back of the house."

"What brought you back here?"

Nels flushed. "Curiosity," he said. "I liked the way he had this place fixed up and I wanted to see the rest of it."

"Do you think Preston was killed before Tommy was, or after?" King asked Maguire.

"The medical examiner may be able to settle that. Twitchell had been dead just about three hours when we came in here. I can't tell that close about this one. Rigor mortis will set in two to four hours after death; it depends upon the chemistry of the individual body, the age, health, how much he bleeds and so on. We'd better get the doctor here as fast as we can. Alex, you go up and phone for him."

"Shall I telephone the theatre?"

"No. Bertini phoned me on Shane's wire; they were just leaving the theatre; the body had gone to Bellevue. They ought to be back in West 20th Street about now. Wait a minute, Alex. Tell the sergeant to send over Arthur Fowler. That Cockney may be of some help if this fellow's an Englishman. With you and me—and Bertini's on his way over—that'll give us four men who were on the case from the first, and that ought to be enough, with Reed. Better get a couple of uniformed men from the precinct, too. The captain and the sergeant will be over, again, and the place will be cluttered up with cops. I don't think there's any doubt these killings will link up. You'd better notify the Commissioner, but tell him I said for him not to bother to come over unless he wants to, see?"

"Yes, sir." Rorty departed.

"It burns me up to think of the time we wasted going through that damn column," Maguire muttered. Nels felt guilty; it had been his idea originally that the murderer's name would be found in the torn column he had picked up near Twitchell's body.

"I don't think it was wasted," King demurred.

"Well, what have we got?" Maguire demanded. "Two hot trails, neither one of them directly out of the column, and two other possibilities, neither of them even named in the column."

"Jack Jordan, Marya Czerna and who else?" King wondered aloud.

"Well, you and the fireman are still in the clear," the inspector said, cryptically.

Footsteps of a man in a hurry came thudding toward them along the carpeted corridor. Sergeant Rorty caught the door jamb to stop himself. His face was crimson.

"Czerna's gone!"

"What?"

"I've been through the whole place, even the bathrooms, except back here—" He whirled and vanished. By the time the three men got to the swinging pantry door, Rorty was emerging through it. "She's not in the kitchen," he said. "She's gone."

"The terrace?" King suggested.

"Door to the roof is locked, inside. She went down the elevator, or more likely down that inside fire escape you get into from the parlor."

"Get downstairs as fast as you can. Put men on all the exits. Get the house manager. . . ." Rorty was on his way. "Come up through the building and search every floor," the inspector called after him. "I'll do the phoning."

"Well," he added, disgust dripping from his words, "there's a swell boner we can't blame on Reed. I've got to go telephone. Be sure you don't touch anything." He stalked out.

The fireman went back into Preston's room, Mr. King following.

"I saw something a while ago," said Nels. "Look. Something was taken out of the tray of that trunk."

King stepped across the legs of the body to look. There was a rectangular space about the size of a packet of letters, at the end of the tray on the right side of the body.

"There's the motive for this murder, anyway," said King. "You've got good eyes, boy."

"I read detective stories all the time," Nels explained, flushing. "I'd like to be a detective instead of a fireman."

"You're the best body and clue finder I ever ran into," said Mr. King, smiling feebly. "The air in here makes me a little sick. I'm going up front."

"Wait. Here's something else. I saw it when I got the towel." Nels pulled Mr. King by the sleeve of his dressing gown and led him past the dead man's feet into the bathroom. On the tiled floor alongside the hand basin stood a huge English kit bag of well-worn brown leather. It was open; it had been packed full of a man's linen and toilet articles.

"He was going somewhere, if this was his. It wasn't Mr. Twitchell's, was it?" Nels asked.

King bent over the huge bag, then knelt beside it. He said: "I'm sure it wasn't Tommy's; all his luggage was pigskin; he had a weakness for anything made of pigskin. Look here—there's some initials under here."

Mr. King moved aside to let the fireman kneel down and peer under the edge of the frame of the opened bag.

"They're pretty dim, but I make them out 'A. P. R.,'" said Mr. King.

"Me too," said Nels.

There was nothing else in the bathroom to merit attention. Nels picked up the soiled towel from the floor where the inspector had flung it and put it in the linen hamper.

"I'd like to know whether he had packed up everything in that dresser," King said, as he stepped over the dead man's legs, "but I suppose we shouldn't touch it." Nevertheless, he walked over, opened the drawers and closed each carefully.

"Empty," he said, "except some old socks and shirts."

At the door he turned for a last look. Nels had stopped at the far side of the trunk and was bent over, peering at the floor.

"There's an old newspaper clipping—some clippings pinned together—at the end of the trunk here," he said.

King came back and bent over it. The yellowed clipping, he recognized by the type and the style of heading, was from an English newspaper.

"Read it," he said. "I can't see fine print in that light without my glasses."

Nels read it aloud, slowly:

GUARDSMAN'S RESIGNATION
Capt. A. P. Ruthven Will Pursue
Career on Stage
One of 'Contemptibles'

The resignation of Captain Alwyn Preston Ruthven, H. M. Foot Guards, Wellington Barracks, is announced to take effect January first.

Mr. Ruthven enlisted August 8, 1914, responding to the first call for volunteers, at the age of 18 yrs, and was sent with the first replacements to join the 'Contemptibles.' He was slightly wounded at Mons and again in 1916 on the Somme. He was commissioned in the infantry in March, 1915. He served as acting battalion commander with the rank of brevet major during the Hundred Days drive that ended the war, with 2nd Battn. King's Own Light Infantry. He joined his present Guards regiment by transfer in 1919. He was twice cited in regimental orders for gallantry in action.

He is the only son of Rev. Alwyn Hal-
lette Ruthven, late rector of St. Mary's in the
Fields, Botsford, Hants and the Honorable
Evelyn T. D. Preston Ruthven, his wife, of
Foxwold, Charnling Wood, Hants, both of
whom died in 1919. During the war and particularly during his service with the Army of
Occupation in the Rhineland, Captain Ruthven was known as a talented amateur actor on
divisional and Army concert parties. He is re-
signing, it is announced, in order to pursue a
professional career on the stage. He has been
appearing of late in repertory with the Chel-
sea Players (amateur) of King's Gate.

"The English write their newspapers funny, don't they?"
Nels commented. "This fellow was a gentleman, all right,
Mr. King, if it's him."

"It's he, all right. He went under the name of Alwyn
Preston here. Do you see any date on that clipping?"

"No, sir." The fireman rose from his knees. "Should we
tell the Inspector about this or wait for him to find it?"

"I'd wait. He's in a pretty short temper, and I have an
idea that this investigation is not going to be so sociable
from now on."

Reluctantly they closed the door behind them and went
forward. As they entered the living room a small, dark
man in a black overcoat, a green felt hat, a chalk-striped
black suit and bright yellow shoes was just being admitted
by the inspector.

"Where's the rest of them?" Maguire demanded.

"They went back to the station. I thought I'd come
over here—maybe you might need me."

"We need you. We just found another stiff back there."

"My God! Who?"

"Twitchell's secretary—or confidential man. Shot. Louie, you know Marya Czerna?"

"Sure. I know her a long time. She's a wop, you know."

"All right. We want her. We had her, but she got away
when we all ran back there to see this dead man. Keep that
under your hat, see? She passed out in here when I told her
Twitchell was dead—he used to be her boy friend—" Louie
nodded, knowingly. "Do you know where to look for her?"

"I'll try, Inspector. It may take two, three days, maybe
more, if she's hidin' out."

"All right. Take it. You start down this fire escape." He
opened the door from the foyer into the inside fire stairway. "No, that won't do; there's no knobs on the outside of
these doors. Well, you go down the elevator—"

"There's a stairway on the far side of the elevator shaft,
opening into the halls, Inspector," Wylie King spoke up.
"Those doors have knobs on both sides; only these doors
that open directly into the apartments haven't. Below the
twenty-fourth floor there's another of these fire escapes,
and below the twelfth there are two more."

"All right, start down, Bertini, and go through every
floor—not into the apartments, of course. You'll meet
Rorty and some others coming up from downstairs. When
you do, tell Rorty to come on up here to me. You go ahead
after Czerna, then, if you haven't found her in the building. Keep in touch with me every couple of hours."

Bertini nodded and went out. Shane O'Neal caught the
door as it was closing and came in. He was out of his tailcoat now and in a green silk moire dressing gown with
dark green velvet facing. He seemed to be dazed. He ran
his fingers through the back of his curly mane of red hair,
as though to make sure that he, too, had not been shot.

"Preston—he's dead too?" he whispered.

"How did you know?" Maguire shot the question at
him sharply.

"The sergeant told me. I was coming in, before, to tell you about Patsy. I had to go back and get another drink. It made me sick, Barney." He groped behind him for one of the low chairs, grasped its metal arm and let himself down gingerly into it.

"When did you last see Preston alive?" Maguire asked.

"About seven. He came in while Tommy was dressing."

"Did you notice anything out of the way about him? Did he seem worried?"

O'Neal thought a moment. "No, quite the reverse. He and Tommy were kidding back and forth."

"Kidding about what?"

"Oh, foolishness. Tommy was kidding him about a date with some girl named Lily."

"Any idea who Lily is?"

"No, Barney. All I got was that she had called up while Preston was out somewhere. Tommy had taken a message for him to call her."

"When had she called up?"

"I don't know. Tommy got in from Long Island, about five o'clock. It was after that. I know he and I got to the Colony at 7:25."

"Was Preston still here when you left?"

"Yes. He rang up the elevator for us and told us good night. He seemed cheerful enough."

King reflected aloud.

"If you'd had the gift of second sight, Shane, and had asked who Lily was, we might know where to turn. Of course, we may get a lead from Preston's letters or his address book."

"How's Patsy?" King inquired. "You said something about her a while ago."

"I got that tight dress off and put her to bed," said Shane, "but she's still giving Reed trouble, wanting to go after Jack Jordan. She's hysterical, sort of."

Shane seemed like a man in a trance: his speech was blurred a bit, too. It came over Nels that Mr. O'Neal had been bolstering up his three o'clock in the morning courage with deep draughts on the whiskey bottle.

"Barney," said King, "I think it would be a good idea, if you're not needing Shane now, for him to turn in, too. Until the medical examiner gets through here there won't be much he can do." He winked at the inspector. "I'll get the house physician to come up and give Miss Paris a sedative, if it's all right with you."

"That's a good idea." The inspector indicated, in dumb show, that O'Neal was not to have anything more to drink.

"I'm all right, Barney," O'Neal objected. "I'm just tired, that's all." But he let Wylie help him out of the deep chair.

"I don't know's I blame the lad for hittin' the bottle," Maguire commented to Nels when the two had gone out. "Singers have nerves like a woman. Shane never did like to see things that were dead or bloody. I took up for him once when some boys from Avenue B was makin' him carry around a cat that'd been run over by a brewery wagon."

"He don't look like a coward," said Nels.

"He ain't. He was just a thin, puny kid. After he got his growth he filled out, and now he's got a fine physique on him. Plays a fine game of handball. He can beat me, hands down."

The inspector was pacing up and down the living room; Nels was leaning against the open archway into the corridor that led to the back of the house and its grisly occupant.

"Have a cigar, fireman?" The inspector wheeled and brought a leather case out of the inside pocket of his dinner coat, now streaked with cigar ashes. Nels thanked him, kindled the cigar from Maguire's lighter, puffed in nervous silence. The detective resumed his pacing. Nels was trying to make some sense of this extra killing.

"Inspector," he asked, "did you notice some papers was missing from the tray of that trunk? At least there was a hole where something had been taken out."

"Yes, I saw that. How long have you been a fireman, boy?"

"Three years. I was in the Bronx, first. I came down to No. 21 last September."

"Didn't you say you'd like to be a detective?"

"I sure would, Inspector."

"You'd have to walk a beat first. It ain't easy on the feet, and it's mighty cold out in the precincts."

"I come from a cold country," said Nels.

"How long you been over here?"

"Since I was sixteen. I'm twenty-five, next month."

"Sweden, eh?"

"Norway."

"What town?"

"We lived in the woods. Lumbering, and a little farm."

"Where'd you learn your English? You speak it fine. None of this 'Ay bane goin' stuff."

"I tried to speak good American from the first. I went to night school."

The telephone interrupted. Maguire went around into Twitchell's office and answered the wrong one, then the right one.

"Who?" he said. "Oh, yes. This is the Inspector. Send him up to me, will you?" He came back.

"Mr. Edwards, who owns the *Evening Blade*. I've been wondering where the hell he was?"

"Me too," said Nels.

The inspector shot him an amused look.

"You've made only one false move all night."

Nels tried to think what that was.

"You let Czerna get away. Even if the rest of us lost our heads, you ought 'a' been out here sitting on her chest when we came back."

"I didn't think of her, Inspector," Nels assured him, guiltily.

"Well, that never came up before since I'm on the force—talking to a suspect, I mean, and have a man come in and say that there was another corpse in the house."

The door buzzer sounded. It was Wylie King returning.

"Shane's lying down on his bed," he said. "He didn't want to undress and I thought maybe he'd better not, anyway. The doctor fixed up Miss Paris so she'll go to sleep."

"You mean the doctor's been there, already? You certainly got him quick."

"He was on the floor below this one, doing the same thing: giving a woman a sedative for her nerves. The desk rang him there and all he had to do was walk up one flight."

"I told you the tenants in this building had bad consciences." Maguire winked at Nels.

"No, this wasn't bad conscience; it was overwork. An actress who has been rehearsing day and night. She—"

Maguire had no more time for gossip. "Mr. Edwards is on his way up," he informed King. He had left open the door into the outer hall.

The elevator door slid open. A dapper, round-faced cherub of a man in a black Chesterfield coat and a soft black hat walked into the foyer. He wore spectacles with invisible shell rims.

"I've been over at the *Blade* office, Wylie," he explained, shaking hands. "I had to go over, because nobody else knew enough about Tommy to handle the story right. I hope I haven't delayed anything." He spoke in a hushed tone, as though he were in the presence of the dead.

"This is Inspector Maguire of the Homicide Squad— Mr. Edwards. Or maybe you know each other." Edwards put out his hand, beaming.

"Barney Maguire, I'm sure glad to meet you. I've been hearing about you ever since I came to the big town." He shook hands vigorously.

"Your friend has Irish blood," said Maguire, twinkling at King. "Come in, Mr. Edwards, and take a chair."

Edwards hung up his coat and hat in the foyer closet and joined them in the living room. He seated himself on the edge of the divan, and spoke, less jauntily. "I just started to say: 'Where the hell is Tommy.'" He got a handkerchief out of the tail pocket of his almost too perfect evening clothes and blew his nose.

"You only know the half of it," said Maguire, gloomily. "You didn't know about Preston?"

"What about him?"

"They got him too."

Edwards looked blank; the fresh color was ebbing out of his face.

"Somebody shot Preston, in his room, back there," Maguire explained.

"Dead?"

"Been dead three hours, I should say. We found him at half after two. The fireman, there—shake hands with Nels Lundberg, Mr. Edwards—Nels smelled something burning and went and found him. Shot from here to here." He indicated the course of the bullet with his forefingers. "He was kneeling over a steamer trunk. He was all right at seven o'clock, when Twitchell and Shane O'Neal left him here to go to dinner."

The publisher looked from one grim face to another of the three.

"You've got no clues at all?" he asked.

"No clue but a torn page from the *Blade* with Twitchell's column on one side of it." He went on to recount how the fireman had found the pieces of it near Twitchell's body.

"May I use the telephone?" Edwards asked, when he had finished.

"If you mean to telephone that to the paper, don't, Mr. Edwards. The clue to the murder may be in that column, and you'd only be giving warning that we're on that trail, see?"

The feelings of a newspaper man with a good story and those of a good citizen and a friend trying to bring a murderer to justice struggled in Edwards' face.

"If you'll give me a few minutes' break on it when you're ready to release it—" he proposed.

"The Commissioner will have to release it," said Maguire.

"Has he got the clipping?"

"It's down at headquarters by now, in the safe. He'll give you a photostatic copy."

"We could fake it, of course," Edwards reminded him, "by tearing a page and making a cut of it."

"Then be sure you get the bloodstains on the right half," said Maguire.

"On the right half of the page?"

"I meant on the half of the page they were on. I'm not putting out any more."

"Well," said Edwards, apologetically, "I was just joking anyway. It's a swell story—man, what a story! But I'll play your way, Inspector. And the opposition will print the clipping tomorrow morning, what'll you bet."

"They might, if they knew about it."

"Who does know about it?"

"Nobody that's going to tell the newspapers."

"Do the papers know about Preston?"

"If they don't, they will, in a little while. The medical examiner's on his way, and the City News man will come along."

Edwards looked at his watch. "It's ten minutes to three," he said. "Why couldn't you have found the body for the afternoon papers, fireman?"

Nels didn't understand him.

"I mean, if you had found him a couple of hours later, you'd have given the afternoon papers a break. I publish the *Evening Blade.*"

Nels smiled politely.

"I don't have to remind you, Mr. Edwards, that you're not here as a reporter but to help the police," Maguire said, formally.

"There's a dozen reporters downstairs that would give a right arm to be up here, under any conditions," Edwards countered. "I'll play ball."

"I'll go down pretty soon and talk to them. Have you got any idea of who might have killed Twitchell—and this Preston?"

"Inspector, there's been a lot of joshing about somebody's taking a shot at Tommy, some day, but I never believed it would happen." He sighed deeply, blew his nose. "May I ask—not as a newspaper man, understand—what lines you are working on?"

"Well," said Maguire, slowly, "we took time to analyze the column before we came in here and found this second body. Then Miss Paris took a shot at Jordan and sort of—"

Edwards was on his feet.

"No, when?" he demanded.

"At the Del Oro, in his office. She went straight over there from your house."

"Did she hit him? Where is she?"

"She hit him—we don't know how bad. They got him away too quick."

Edwards looked from one to the other for confirmation.

"Why, I left the *Blade* office not fifteen minutes ago," he protested, "and they didn't know anything about Jordan's being shot! Wait—there was a tip on the ticker that some girl tried to shoot herself in the Del Oro, but the city desk couldn't get anything out of the management. We didn't have a man to send over there, at this hour of the morning, with the Twitchell story under way. We had no idea it linked up with this. Couldn't I telephone about that?"

"That Jordan bunch covers up pretty fast," said the inspector, evading the question. "They said Jordan went to a doctor, but we haven't found him yet. At three o'clock we're sending the customers home and taking the whole staff over to West Forty-seventh Street Station for a little inquiry. We want Jordan. I don't mind telling you that we want to ask him about Twitchell's murder. Keep that under your hat, too, will you, please?"

"Is that why Patsy—"

"That was why. She went off half-cocked, but she was sure it was him that killed Tommy." Maguire went on to tell what had happened after the dancer had disappeared from Edwards' apartment, ending with the assurance that she was now safely asleep in Shane O'Neal's guest room.

"She's under arrest, of course?" Edwards asked.

"About four ways," said Maguire, drily.

"What else have you got on Jordan?"

King told him about having seen Jordan come out of the theatre.

"But that doesn't prove anything," he concluded. "He was probably just taking his car around to park it near the stage door, to be ready for Patsy."

"Then there's Marya Czerna," the inspector resumed. "Did you know about her going for Twitchell with a knife here a couple of months ago?"

Edwards nodded. "Tommy told me. What else have you got on her?"

"She was at the theatre tonight; she left a little early; I spoke to her coming out and sent a man to trail her. She went to the Del Oro. She disappeared from there—gave my man the slip—after her first show and just before Miss Paris shot at Jordan. An hour after that she phoned over here to warn Tommy to stay away from Jordan. King told her to come on over. And she did. Then she pretended she didn't know Tommy was dead. She keeled over on the lounge, and just then the fireman sprung it on us that Preston was in the back room. We all went tearing back there and Czerna flew the coop. We figure she went down the fire escape—it's an inside one. I've got two men going through the building, but I don't hope to get her that easy."

Edwards shook his head in agreement. "No, you won't for a while," he said, drily. "She's long gone from here. I can tell you that."

"Why?"

"I came in by the service entrance, so the newspaper boys in the lobby wouldn't see me. Just as I came in Marya went out. She passed me so fast she didn't recognize me, I guess, and I didn't think about stopping her until she was gone. Then I went out on the sidewalk. There was a cab in the middle of the street. Its door slammed and it turned south on Sixth Avenue in a hurry. I suppose she was in it."

Maguire snapped his fingers.

"You didn't get the number of the cab?"

"I didn't think to. All I wanted of her was to say something to her about Tommy. It didn't cross my mind then that the police would be after her."

"Well, that's that!" said King, disgusted.

"Do you think she shot him? It doesn't seem possible in a public place like that."

"If she shot him, she did it on the impulse, Mr. Edwards," the inspector pontificated. He paused.

"That's how women kill men. They don't pick their spots in advance; you ought to know that by this time. We've got a motive on her—jealousy. That's the best possible motive for a woman. But, you know, I don't believe she killed him, either." He looked around at his auditors as though defying them to disagree. "If she was faking here a while ago, she's an actress to beat Bernhardt."

Edwards nodded.

"We haven't got a real motive for Jordan's knocking him off." The inspector resumed his pacing. "You don't kill a man just because you want his girl—particularly when she's been sitting on your lap and sort of promising that there may be something doing. No, if Jordan shot him he did it for some reason that hasn't come out."

"His pursuing Patsy might have been part of a campaign against Tommy," King suggested.

"It might," Maguire agreed. "But then where does this fellow Preston come into the picture?"

"Could Jordan or Czerna or both of them in cahoots have sent a gorilla up here who got Preston by mistake?" Edwards suggested.

"They didn't look anything alike," Maguire reminded him. "Whoever killed Preston was let in by Preston and went with him back to his room, presumably to get something out of the trunk. Of course, Preston may have had a cannon in his ribs from the moment he let this party in, but I don't think so. A man don't keep on smoking a cigar when there's a gun at his back. There's a space empty in the trunk tray that looks like a package, maybe of letters, was taken out. There's a motive for you."

"How do you know he was smoking a cigar?" Edwards asked.

"His head fell on the edge of the bed—he was bending over this steamer trunk on his knees—and the cigar set the bedclothes afire—"

"Could I take a look at it?" Edwards asked. "I'm a little mixed up—"

"Sure, come on back."

King and the fireman waited in the living room.

Presently the two returned.

"Suppose you and Mr. Edwards go into Shane's place and let him look over that column," the inspector suggested to King, practically making it a command. "This place'll be so full of my men in a few minutes that you can't hear yourself think. I'll be in there after I get things started here. What I want to know is whether Mr. Edwards can throw any light on anyone named in that column who'd be likely to have gone after Twitchell."

"You can be glad he didn't have as many names as he usually does on Mondays," King said. "You'll have a sweet mess, as it is, when you come to check up."

"The gossip crop has been pretty thin since New Year's," Edwards admitted. "Tommy was slowing up, too; he needed a vacation. If he had only listened to me he'd be lying somewhere on a beach in the sunshine instead—" He broke off.

The telephone was ringing in the office. The inspector was on his way to answer it.

"Yes," they heard him say. "I sent for them. Yes, him too. We want to make some pictures up here. . . . No, not for the newspapers. . . . Is that so? Well, tell them he's up here as a witness and not as a newspaper man, and they can take my word on that. I'll be down in a few minutes and tell them all about it. I want to talk to you when I come down. . . . Well, we'll take one thing at a time. . . . Thanks."

Inspector Maguire came back into the room, head bent, tugging at his short moustache.

"The medical examiner is here, and the newspaper men want to know about Preston. I'll go down and tell them as soon as the doctor gets to work."

He snapped his fingers, turned, walked back toward the telephone.

The telephone was ringing again before he got to it. It was not the house telephone, this time, but Twitchell's private line.

"Yes. This is him . . ." There was a considerable pause.

"Say that again, will you? I didn't get you? Say it again."

His voice dropped until it was barely audible in the next room. He was repeating a street address, but Nels couldn't catch it, except the words "West Fifty-fourth." There was further low questioning, a sharp "Hello! . . . Hello!" They heard him complain to the operator that he had been cut off, heard him tell her who he was and order her to get the number of the telephone that had just called him. He had to talk to the chief operator, who evidently promised to report later.

When he came back into the living room, King, Edwards, and the fireman were standing up waiting for him.

"This is sure a windowful of nuts," he declared. "A party says if I'll go to a place over on West Fifty-fourth Street beyond Tenth Avenue I'll find Jack Jordan in the third floor flat. And do you know who I think it was?"

They waited.

"She had a deep voice and a wop accent, but they both sounded phony. I may be wrong, but I think it was Marya Czerna."

7

Nels tried to make himself inconspicuous as the two gentlemen left by the hall door to go over to the O'Neal apartment, but the inspector spied him.

"You better go along, fireman," he suggested, more preoccupied than polite. "This place will be cluttered up with high-powered detectives in a few minutes."

Nels saluted dejectedly and hastened after Mr. King and Mr. Edwards. For the first time since he had found Twitchell's body, Nels was deprived of his front row seat at the drama of tracking down the murderer. It was only by luck he had been enabled to see this much, instead of being sent back to the engine house, but that philosophic reflection didn't lessen his disappointment a bit. This Preston murder the fireman had begun to regard as his own case. He and Mr. King had turned up the only four clues so far found in this new puzzle. Now he was out of it.

At the desk, King and Edwards were murmuring over clippings of the Twitchell column. Standing in front of the fireplace, after he had mended the fire, Nels couldn't hear a word they were saying. He moved to the chair nearest them; still he couldn't hear; this room was too big. All he could do was sit and let his thoughts run wild.

Where was Miss Paris? And Mr. O'Neal? He got up and catfooted to the corridor archway. In the corridor, on a chair planted between two doors, was Detective Reed, stolidly reading a pink tabloid. He looked up, none too cordially, when Nels tiptoed up to him.

"Where's Mr. O'Neal?" he asked, in a whisper.

The detective indicated one door with a jerk of his head. "Asleep," he said. "Too much outa the bottle. He passed out."

"Where's the young lady?"

Reed indicated the other door with a thumb. "Dead to the world," he said. "The doctor give her a shot of something. Sleepin' like a baby. I ain't sorry, lemme tell you. She's a young hell cat." He modified this rash statement, hastily, seeing the fireman's face. "I don't mean she's bad, understand me, but she fights dirty." He went back to reading his paper.

Nels went back and mended the fire again, needlessly. That left him with nothing to do.

He worked up courage to disturb Mr. King and Mr. Edwards and asked for some paper from the desk. He went back to the piano bench Sergeant Rorty had occupied while taking notes during the analysis of the column. He began to set down, carefully, the suspects and the clews he could muster. After thirty minutes he read over his list:

SUSPECTS

Jack Jordan

Marya Czerna

P. Paris

Shane O'Neal

Anyone of 20 people named in the column

Reasons for Jordan—trying to make Miss Paris for two months. Made threats against T. in her dressing room before I found T.'s body. Had pistol on him last night, P. Paris says.

Reasons against J.—Why should he have snatched column away from T. and torn it? Why should he kill Preston? How did he get into this apartment to kill P.?

Reasons for Czerna—Jealous over Miss Paris and T. Tried to stab T. day after Thanksgiving.

Reasons against her—Why would she kill Preston? Why would she call T. up at his apt. and come over here and faint when Insp. told her T. was dead? (Unless she was trying to throw off suspicion maybe.)

Reasons for Miss Paris—Had pistol. Maybe had it when she was at theatre. Was late getting dressed for second act. Could she have been downstairs in lounge at time T. was shot? Left theatre early and could have come here and killed Preston (Boloney).

Reasons against Miss Paris—No motive I know of. She loved T. and was going to marry him. Does not look like killing kind of girl but she was going to kill Jordan and did shoot him. (??)

Reasons for Shane O'Neal—He is in love with P. P. Was out of his seat we don't know how long after start of second act. Says he was looking for T. to give him P.'s note.

Reasons against O'Neal—not a killer. Too kind hearted. No real motive for killing his friend that we know of.

People in column—I still think murderer is in it but I don't know enough about these people yet.

THINGS TO FIND OUT

Did anybody see anybody come up to the penthouses bet. 7 p.m. when T. and O'Neal went to dinner and time we came up (about 12:30 a.m.)?

Did doormen or elevator men see J. Jordan, M.
    Czerna, P. Paris, S. O'Neal or anybody named in
    column come into Park Tower during that time?
How did Captain Ruthven come to be secretary to
    T. T.?
Where was he going that he packed his bag and
    trunk?
Who was Lily that telephoned T. to have P. call her
    last night?
What other women did P. go around with?
Who were his men friends?
Who was the woman who was crying in tel. booth at
    theatre after I found body of T.? Probably noth-
    ing to do with this. Remind Insp.

He dated the list at the bottom: 3:30 a.m. Tuesday,
January 27, 1931.

Someone was standing behind Nels. He looked around. It
was Mr. King.

"What have you been doing there?" King asked, his eyes
smiling over the half-moon lenses of his reading glasses.

"I thought I'd stop and write down what I know about
these murders and maybe I could tell what to do next,"
Nels explained. He knew he was blushing.

"Do you mind if I look at it?" The little man looked
like a benign schoolmaster in those spectacles. Even under this strain, Mr. King had not lost his humor nor his
charm.

He studied the two sheets of notes in the fireman's
careful, round script. He walked across the big room to
the desk where the publisher was still poring over the clipping of the column.

"Ted," he said, "here's a feature for you. Sign up this
lad over here to do a first-person story. He found both

bodies, he picked up the torn column, and he's a demon at uncovering clues."

Nels, alarmed, had followed him over.

"Mr. King, I don't suspect Miss Paris or Mr. O'Neal. I just put them down because you shouldn't overlook anybody who could have done the crime."

"Then why did you overlook me?" Mr. King asked, his face quite serious. "I left the theatre, or I say I did, before you found the body. And I'm in love with the young lady, too."

"I knew that," said Nels, just as gravely. He reached for his list, but Mr. Edwards held off his hand.

"That's a fine idea, Wylie. How about it, fireman?"

"How about what, Mr. Edwards?"

"How about giving the *Blade* an exclusive story on your part in this?"

Nels swallowed. "I'd have to ask the Inspector, and the captain."

"What captain?"

"The captain of my fire company. I don't want to lose my job."

"Oh, I can arrange that," said the publisher.

"Well, if you can fix it, it's all right with me," Nels decided. "Only I'm not much of a writer."

"We'll attend to the writing. You just tell your story in your own words to one of my young men. I'll give you a hundred dollars for it."

"Gee!" said Nels.

"He'll give you two hundred and fifty dollars for it, or we'll sell it to the opposition," Mr. King spoke up. "I'm your agent, Nels."

"Okay," said Nels, grinning.

"You dirty gyp!" said Edwards to Mr. King. "I'll give you at least a hundred dollars, Nels for a thousand words, and if it's good enough to run longer, I'll pay you at the same rate."

"Whatever you say," Nels agreed. "Could I see your list?"

"We just listed the people in the column," Edwards said, passing over the two sheets of paper covered with King's copperplate writing. He fell to studying the fireman's list.

Nels took the other men's notes across to his bench, under the piano lamp. The top page was headed:

ELIMINATED

The banker—probably a gag.

The Lester Shipps—in Hollywood.

Basil Mollineaux and Eden Hughes—married in S. F. last Friday.

Constance Mollineaux—no cause for offense. Probably abroad now.

Cora Blaisdell Brotherton—in Reno.

The Oklahoma Mamma—Sailed for Europe Friday night.

John Gant and Claire Rivoli—no offense.

Rita Ahearn—good publicity for her.

Constance Crain—press agent item.

Alice de Kosla—in Reno.

Gene Mahoney—just kidding.

Manfred Wagenaar and his first wife—abroad.

Alpert and Torres—item true and harmless.

Peggy Royce—loves any kind of publicity.

Karyl Wilde—ditto and double it.

Hazel Dameron—another attention caller.

Lorna Boone—ditto.

Lisbeth Lansing—dirty dig at the boy friend, but she'd think it funny.

Caroline Clayton—her idea of privacy is Atlantic City.

The next sheet was headed:

SEEN AT THE WILDE OPENING

Greta Land.

Chubby Chalfonte.

Dorothy Bardling—drunk and cursing Twitchell, but that would be about all.

Cornelius Brotherton and the blonde—too happy to care.

Happy Carewe—drunk but amiable. Talked to fireman in lounge.

Mary May—on the stage.

Marya Czerna.

Jack Jordan.

Big Manny Murillo—no cause for offense in that old chestnut about him. Might be something in the next item on N. Y.-Chicago gang merger.

Harvey Thatcher and Alice Adorable.

IMPROBABLE

Mrs. Chalfonte—too much of a lady.

The Raymond Canadays—no offense.

Frank Stayton and Merrill O'Malley—used to Broadway idea of privacy.

Gerald Mudie and the sculptress—up in Westport buried in the snow and each other.

TO INVESTIGATE FIRST

Jack Jordan.

Marya Czerna.

Dorothy Bardling.

Big Manny Murillo.

Harvey Thatcher—though Oklahomans kill their men in public.

Lucia Morena (Sneedon)—hysterical type, and bitter about Wagenaar's leaving her.

"Perhaps you'd better add Shane and me to that last part of my list," King twitted the fireman.

"I meant no offense putting Mr. O'Neal and Miss Paris on mine," Nels assured him again, earnestly. "It's just a rule in murder mysteries that you shouldn't think anyone is innocent until you've found the guilty party."

"Don't let me kid you, Nels," said King.

"And now that we've got these lists, Wylie, what are we going to do with them?" Edwards demanded. "I don't think they prove a thing."

"No more do I," King admitted.

"Why did anybody get the idea that the solution was in this column?" Edwards asked, still studying Nels' list.

"Well, considering that Nels found the two pieces of the page—"

"Oh, yes, to be sure. How do you know it was torn in a struggle, Nels?"

"I'd bet my last dime on that," said Nels, positively. "And if the clipping had nothing to do with the murder how else would you explain that I found one piece wadded up on the floor by the sand jar and the other piece under Mr. Twitchell's feet in the booth?"

Edwards shook his head. "I can't explain it," he admitted. "Well, gentlemen, my guess, not for publication, is Marya Czerna."

"Why?"

"Jealousy. Threats. Previous attempt to stab him. She goes to him with the item about the cooch dance in yesterday's column, picks a quarrel with him, shoots him. On impulse, I mean—not deliberately."

"And then comes all the way from the New Netherland up here—where she's well known to every doorman, elevator man, page and attendant in the house, don't forget—comes up to the penthouse and shoots Preston. And why?" King scoffed.

"You've got me," said Edwards, blankly. "Maybe the Preston shooting had nothing to do with Tommy's."

"If it didn't—don't be absurd, man."

"I'd better leave the detective work to experts. By the way, Wylie, the *Blade* is offering a $10,000 cash reward for information leading to the arrest of the murderer of Tommy Twitchell, payable upon confession or conviction."

"That was a good idea, Ted," said King gravely.

"If it's not enough to get action, we'll raise it, five thousand at a time."

"Better not tell anybody that, or the murderer will die while they're waiting for more money. This is New York, Ted, where justice is blind but foresighted."

"By the way, Wylie, there's one item at the end that I didn't get. Who is the unemployed apple of Lisbeth Lansing's eye?"

"Tracy Millman. He's out of pictures until the silents come back, if ever. He lisps. That was a dirty dig Tommy gave him, but nobody likes him, along the Street. He's the village bore, talking about his departed glories. And he never pays a check."

"Poor devil! What did he do with all his money?"

"Spent it being a great man. Actors are only slightly less brilliant than penguins, Ted."

The telephone behind the tapestry on the wall was whirring. King walked around the desk to answer it as he delivered his opinion of actors.

Detective Luigi Bertini, who had been sent out to find Marya Czerna after her escape, wanted to speak to Inspector Maguire.

"You can call him on Twitchell's private wire; he's in there," King said. Edwards halted him, making signals of protest with his hands.

"Get him in here," he entreated King, in a stage whisper. "I want to know what's going on."

"Hold the wire, Bertini, and I'll go around and get him. I don't remember the number of that telephone. . . . No, it's no trouble at all. Just hang on."

Inspector Maguire came in ahead of King. Edwards was absorbed in something on the desk, which was within arm's reach of the niche in the wall that held both the house phone and the private line instrument.

Judging by the inspector's questions, Bertini had not found Marya. The inspector listened more than he talked. His final instructions were: "Keep after her and keep me posted. I'll be here for several hours yet, the way it looks now. But call me on the wire in Twitchell's place, will you." He gave the detective Twitchell's private number, out of his notebook.

"What's going on, Barney?" King asked. "We're marooned in here and clear out of it."

The inspector, who had headed for the door, halted and came the few steps back.

"This is no *kaffe klatsch*, you know," he said, sharply. "We've spent all too much time now on gossip."

King didn't like that.

"You're trying to catch the murderer of a gossip, Barney. Maybe you'd better bait your hook with all the gossip you can get."

"Don't get me wrong, Wylie," said the big fellow. "You've been invaluable, and you know it. I guess my temper's pretty short. The place is overrun with cops in there and we're not getting anywhere."

"You didn't expect to catch the murderer tonight, did you?" Edwards inquired, a shade sarcastically.

"Well, maybe we've already caught him. But getting evidence to—"

"Who?" King and Edwards said it together.

"Jordan's on his way to Bellevue now."

"How'd you get him?"

"We sent over a wagonload of men to that place on West Fifty-fourth, but all we needed was an ambulance."

"What do you mean?" Both were on their feet.

"He was in the third-floor flat of one of those old brownstones past Tenth Avenue. They had to break in a couple of doors, but there was nobody to stop them. He was all by himself, in bed in the middle room. If anybody was with him, they went out when we started pounding."

"Didn't you have the house surrounded?"

"Sure—if anybody was with Jordan, he just evaporated."

"What did he have to say—Jordan, I mean?" King pursued.

"He was unconscious."

"Is he likely to die?"

"We don't know yet. He'd been fixed up pretty well by a surgeon. There was only one hole in him, through the right shoulder just above the top of the lung. It missed the shoulder blade, going out, or it would have torn him up worse."

"For Patsy's sake, let's hope he gets well," King said, slowly.

"Yes, if he dies, it'll be bad for her."

"Have you found anything more in there—about Preston?"

"Well, we think his name was something else—and you're right about his being a gentleman."

"You mean you found the clippings on the floor. The fireman and I saw that."

Maguire glared at him. "I told you boys not to touch anything—"

"We didn't, Barney. We just stooped over and read the top one," King assured him, maliciously. "And we found the initials on the packed bag. We didn't touch that either."

"You're too damned smart," said Maguire, forced to smile.

"What else did you find, Barney?"

"Well, we found a picture of him with a girl. Maybe you'll tell me she was this—what's her name?—Lily."

"I'd have to see it, first," King suggested.

"Look all you like."

The inspector brought a picture out of the inner pocket of his dinner coat. It was a mounted cabinet photograph with the photographer's name on the mount: "Harrell & Son—No. 15 King's Road." King studied the photograph under the desk lamp with Edwards craning over his shoulder.

"The gent in the morning coat is Preston all right— Captain Alwyn Preston Ruthven, late of His Majesty's Foot Guards." King studied it a minute.

"I think I've seen that girl, somewhere," he hazarded, finally.

"Who is she?" Maguire was no longer sarcastic.

"I'm supposed to have a demon's memory for faces—"

"Women's faces, anyway, Wylie," Edwards twitted him. "If she showed her legs in that picture, Inspector, I'll bet he'd recognize her."

"This is a bride and groom picture, if I'm any judge," King announced.

"I thought that, myself, and so did a couple of the boys."

"There's hardly any doubt of it. Ruthven was a gentleman, too, or the girl would be standing up and he'd be sitting on the marble bench."

"There's no date on it," said Maguire.

"By the style of the lady's dress, I should say 1919 or 1920," King decided. "Moreover, she's not dowdy. Maybe she was an American. She was certainly a sugar plum, whoever she was. Well, now we look for a woman with black hair and dark eyes. That simplifies everything."

Maguire snorted. "You'd crack wise at a funeral!"

"I don't know of a better place to do it," King countered, looking up from the picture. "I suppose you never got drunk and raised hell at a wake, Barney. The best escape mechanism for grief."

"Well, Wylie," said the long-suffering inspector, "if you can't rap the dame suppose you give me back the picture."

"Let me keep it a while—she looks like Adam's second wife. What a honey she was!"

"I'll tell you something practical to do about it," Edwards spoke up. "Print it in the *Blade* and maybe some reader will identify the girl."

"That'll be up to the Commissioner," Maguire said. "I was going to suggest to him that we give the picture to all the papers and press services, especially in England."

"Check," said King, grinning at the publisher, who was trying to appear guileless.

Edwards shrugged his shoulders. "Is it all right with you if I get the fireman, here, to write us a story on how he found the bodies?"

Maguire considered. "Better let me ask the Commissioner," he concluded.

"When are you going to see the Commissioner?"

"He's in there now."

Edwards got to his feet with alacrity. "I'll ask him, myself, if that's all right with you."

"Sure, go ahead."

As the publisher went out through the foyer door into the elevator hall, a man whom neither King nor Nels had seen before came in hurriedly.

"Inspector, the Commissioner would like to see you," he announced, and started back.

"Excuse me." Maguire hastened after him, leaving the picture on the desk. Nels saw Mr. King pick it up and thrust it into the pocket of his dressing gown.

"Who did you mean by Adam's second wife?" Nels asked.

"Her name was Lilith. She came over from the Land of Nod and vamped Adam. She was the mother of all mischief and the patron saint of the motion picture. You see, Nels, she was the original of the Other Woman, without whom there would be no movies. I've been trying for years to get Ponderous to name a theatre for her. We owe it to her memory."

Nels couldn't decide whether this odd sentimental cynic was in earnest. He had never heard of Lilith.

"The pattern story for a box-office feature picture, Nels, is in the second, third and fourth chapters of Genesis. You don't remember reading anything about Lilith in it because the King James translators left out that legend. But there's the perfect screen drama, in three cycles and seven situations: Innocence, idyllic love, temptation, sin, murder, exile and remorse. Let me give you a tip, Nels: read the Bible as literature. It's still far and away the greatest book ever written."

"That's what the English teacher in night school said. If you say so, too, Mr. King, it must be so. Do you ever write books?"

"Not me," said the little man, wryly. "I'm too busy living."

The door buzzer was whirring. Nels opened the door. It was Edwards, with his hat and coat on.

"I've got the Commissioner's permission for you to write your story," he announced. "Will you come along with me over to the *Blade* office?"

"What about my captain's permission?" Nels demurred.

"I'll get that. What are you going to do now, Wylie?"

"Lie down on that divan and try to think. What did the Commissioner say about printing the picture of Preston and the girl?"

"Nothing doing, yet. He may release it to everybody later. Anyway, Maguire's got it, and he's gone downstairs."

Mr. King had the picture in his pocket, but he said nothing. Neither did Nels.

A taxicab rushing through the biting cold across the blue-white, nearly deserted Broadway belt brought them to the *Blade* office in ten minutes.

After he had signed his name in the artist's ink on a piece of white cardboard and had been posed for a flash-light, seated at a desk before a typewriter he couldn't oper-ate, Nels was ushered into a cluttered office in one corner of the spidery loft of the *Blade's* editorial floor. A middle-aged, eye-weary, world-weary, profane and charming fel-low named Dan Flint was to help the fireman tell his story "in his own words." With the aid of a pint of rye whis-key, which he offered to share, and an endless chain of shrewd questions and suggestions, in less than two hours Mr. Flint produced a typewriter sonata he pronounced "a knockout."

"How many columns will it be?" Nels wanted to know.

"Runs about fifteen hundred words. Read it over."

It read astonishingly like the way Nels had told it.

"What did they want me to sign my name for when I came in?"

"So they can reproduce your signature at the head of your piece."

"Did they get the captain's permission?" Nels wanted to know now.

"Edwards tended to that himself. I'll take this out to the desk. You go into his office—the center door at the far end. Thanks, old scout."

Nels sat down to wait for the publisher. It was an elegant office to be in such an old dump of a building. In about ten minutes the little man bustled in.

"That was great stuff, Nels," he said, cordially. "The check will be for two hundred."

"Two hundred words?"

"No, two hundred dollars." Nels swallowed, hard.

"Thanks. Did you ask the captain? I don't want to lose my job."

"He said it was all right, only not to spoil a good fireman."

Nels grinned and blushed. A boy came in without knocking, and with that peculiar lack of respect or awe which comes to its finest democratic flower in newspaper copy boys, nonchalantly dumped into a tray on the publisher's elegant desk a sheaf of letters.

"You get mail at this time of the morning?" Nels commented.

"We get mail every hour—send after it. If you'll wait a few minutes, Nels, I'll be going back over to the Park Tower and I'll take you. I promised to bring you back by six o'clock and let the other newspaper men interview you. But you are not to sign any stories for them, understand. That's our agreement. And don't remember too much for them."

Mr. Edwards was opening his letters with an ivory paper knife. He still had on his hat; his overcoat was flung across a chair.

A queer look passed across his round face as he unfolded one letter.

"Look at this!" he said. Nels got up and moved around to look over his shoulder.

Typewritten on an *Evening Blade* letterhead, it was addressed to Mr. Edwards as publisher of the Blade and was dated "Monday 6 p.m. Jan. 26, 1931." It said:

> "My dear Mr. Edwards:
> "Returning from a week-end on Long Island this afternoon, I bought a copy of the *Blade* at the Penn Station and read my today's column. As you know, I left town on Sunday morning

and for once did not read proof on the Monday column. I could not get a *Blade* in Greenport: the newsdealer there says he cannot get enough copies on Monday.

"In the column I found an item that I did not write, and that certainly was inserted by someone without consulting me. The item happened to be of an inconsequential and non-libelous nature. I am not protesting against it, particularly, but I am most decidedly protesting against the laxness of the copy desk in allowing anything to be inserted in the column without my okay.

"Will you kindly call to the attention of all concerned that my contract with the *Blade* specifically states that not even you as publisher have the privilege of inserting anything in the column, although you have the final say-so on what shall not be run for reasons of policy or on advice of your libel attorneys?

"I am sure that you and my co-workers on the *Blade* will understand that it is no mistaken idea of my own importance or infallibility that makes me complain of this. Once before, about two months ago, an item was inserted. It happened to concern the same person, but because it seemed harmless I let it pass.

"In the eyes of the readers and of persons mentioned in the column I am responsible for every word in it. I am and should be. If I allowed this second offense to pass without protest we might all find ourselves in a serious jam one day.

"Respectfully,

"Tommy Twitchell."

P. S. "Please give Mr. MacInness written instructions that hereafter no page of mine is to be locked up until I have personally read the revised galleys and initialed the proofs. This means giving up occasional week-ends out of town, which are worth while for the news I gather. If I go on vacation, we can make some other arrangement."

Attached by a clip to the top of the letter was a note, also typewritten:

"Ted: I wrote the attached letter so it could be passed around with your order, if you like. I tried to get you by telephone when I got back to town a while ago, but you were out. I'll tell you when I see you what the item was. It was so innocuous that to have quoted it would have made my protest seem foolish.
"T. T."

"If you can find out what the item was that was put in," Nels suggested, "it might have something to do with this case."

"That's what I was thinking. Still, he says here the item was harmless."

"I don't suppose there's any way you can tell which one it was?"

"Certainly there is! Wait! I'll get his copy." He moved his fingers to push a button on the desk, but got up instead and hurried out.

Nels read over Twitchell's letter and note time after time. Mr. Edwards was gone quite a while. When he returned, he appeared to be puzzled and crestfallen. He had some papers in his hand.

"There wasn't any item inserted," he declared.

"Are you sure?"

"Look for yourself." He tossed some news print paper, longer than regular letter size, onto the desk.

"There's not a line inserted anywhere in those four pages," he complained.

There certainly wasn't. Here and there a word or phrase had been blocked out with a row of xxxxxxx's and another word or so typed in between the double-spaced lines, but certainly no complete item had been inserted.

"This looks like he wrote it himself," Nels said. "I mean it's not neat like a stenographer would write it."

"He wrote his copy on his own machine. Sometimes he'd send in extra items in his handwriting, by messenger. Once in a while he'd telephone in a hot one just before press time. But he would never give an item by phone except to one of two men on the copy desk. One of them's on the desk out there now; he says Tommy didn't either send or phone anything all day Sunday. I got the other man out of bed—he works on the night side—and he said Tommy telephoned in three items from Long Island at ten o'clock Saturday night. He was positive it was Tommy; couldn't be any doubt of it. They even joshed about something personal that only Tommy would have known about, he said."

"What were the items he telephoned in?" Nels asked.

"The one about the Leslie Shipps' separation—they're out in Hollywood, but she's from that Long Island set he was week-ending with; the one about the Ray Canadays getting a Mexican divorce and the one on John Gant and Claire Rivoli. Eddie read 'em all back to Tommy, so he knows they were all right."

Nels couldn't see any way around that, but the publisher could.

"We'll go back over there and lay this before the Commissioner and Maguire. Maybe we can find the copy of the *Blade* that Tommy bought at the Penn Station when he got back to town. He might have made a pencil mark on the item he's complaining about. It's a long shot, but we might as well try it."

He gathered up the letter, the sheets of Twitchell's copy and his overcoat and headed for the door, with Nels behind him.

A bald man in shirt sleeves was just coming into the office.

"Mr. Edwards," he said, "the police have given out a statement that they are holding this racketeer, Jack Jordan, for questioning in the Twitchell case. He's recovered consciousness and he's raising hell at Bellevue, Wally says, because they can't find his lawyer."

"What does he say about the Twitchell killing?"

"He denies all knowledge of it. And he's running true to gangster form. He won't say who shot him."

"Didn't they tell him that Miss Paris confessed to it?"

"The Commissioner did, and all he'd say was: 'She's crazy. She's trying to cover up somebody. I ought to know who shot me. It wasn't that kid. She's crazy.'" He was reading the quotation from a sheet of carbon copy in his hand. Edwards took it from him, read it carefully.

"Somebody's crazy!" he said, handing it back. "Well, remember what I said: we're not going to hound Miss Paris. Keep your story fair to her. If she did shoot him, she ought to have a medal for it, and so far no charges have been filed against her."

"Where is she? The police say she is being held as a witness, but they won't say where they've got her."

Edwards' eyes twitched behind his round spectacles. He looked at Nels.

"Keep on trying to find her," he said, curtly and unnecessarily. "If you want me for anything you can get me at Twitchell's private number. I'll either be there or in Shane

O'Neal's apartment next door in the penthouse. And don't let the makeup cut a line of my story about Twitchell." He turned to make for the elevator.

The taxicab sped through the cold grey of the milk-man's hour. Times Square, its galaxy of lights extinguished, looked like the slum it really is. Edwards and the fireman were silent all the way across and up town.

Brakes screaming, the cab slid into the curb at the Park Tower just behind another taxi. They clambered out, Edwards swearing under his breath. Their driver was cursing, too, not under his breath.

From the cab ahead descended a little man in a black overcoat, a green hat—Bertini! After him emerged a blonde girl in a sable coat—Marya Czerna!

Bertini lifted her out of the cab, though she was taller than he. A policeman who had alighted on the other side came hastening around to relieve the little detective of his burden. Bertini was paying off the cab now and had not yet seen Edwards and the fireman; Mr. Edwards was paying his driver and had not recognized the others.

The regal platinum head was bobbing over the big bluecoat's shoulder like a baby's in arms. Mr. Edwards had turned now and was blinking at her, open-mouthed.

"Hi, Ted!" she greeted him, hysterically shrill.

Her feet and lower legs protruded, stiffly, on the other side of the policeman. She had on loose felt slippers and no stockings; both ankles were bound in gauze bandage and tape.

"Where have you been?" Edwards demanded, taken aback.

"She's been jumpin' off fire escapes," said the police-man, sourly. "Stop wigglin', sister, or I'll drop you on them lame puppies."

8

"Take her in," Bertini instructed the patrolman.

Bystanders seemed to be springing up out of manholes, materializing from jets of steam that curled up from the power mains under the street, or taking form from the coal smoke that poured into the shivering dawn from a myriad chimneys. Where else could they have come from so suddenly at six o'clock of a bitter cold morning in this street?

The five hurried through the lobby into an elevator, whose door shut in the faces of half a dozen legmen from the press on watch in the lobby: Marya cradled in the arms of the bluecoat, the terrier-like detective, the cherubic Edwards, the grave blond giant, Nels the fireman. At the penthouse level a policeman on guard sat on the hall divan. He got up, gave the embarrassed patrolman carrying Marya a leer and a wink. Bertini thumbed the button on the door that had been Tommy Twitchell's.

Detective Fowler admitted them. The policeman set his burden of beauty down on the semi-circular black and silver striped divan, carefully. She was a lovely thing, certainly, Nels had to admit, though he did not care for blondes. But this one was all woman, all fire, all grace, all seduction.

Fowler had disappeared toward the rear of the apartment. Inspector Maguire appeared from the back regions.

He had taken off his collar and tie; his dinner coat and black silk waistcoat were smudged with cigar ashes.

"Where did you get her, Louie?" he asked, disregarding Marya, who lay on the divan with her eyes closed.

"We went to the Del Oro and got the list of the girls in their show and their addresses," Bertini explained. "The third place we went, she was there. Up in West Sixty-ninth Street with a kid they call Tanya."

"How'd she hurt her ankles?"

"Droppin' off the fire escape at the back. She hung by her hands and only had to drop six feet into the court, but she didn't know enough to take off them high-heeled shoes first."

Marya, lying back on pillows on the couch, managed a twisted grin. Nels noticed that she had removed the heavy night club makeup since they had last seen her.

"He knows everything, that Bertini," the night club hostess said ruefully, without opening her eyes. She had been drinking, and too much.

"How bad are the ankles?" Maguire wanted to know.

"Not bad. Just wrenched. There was only two of us— Mullanphy and me. She might have got away if she hadn't twisted 'em. We went down the fire escape after her. I never know there was so many cuss words in the Italian language."

Marya's brown eyes glared at him.

"Well, what are you going to do about me?" she quizzed the inspector, as jauntily as she could manage.

"Lock you up, when we get through with you."

"What have I done?" she demanded.

"You're a material witness, to say the least. The sooner you tell me everything you know, the sooner you'll know what we're going to do with you."

She gave him a smile of slow scorn.

"I've got too many friends in this town that can tell you where to head in, Barney Maguire—"

"Your friends won't help you much when we charge you with the murder of Tommy Twitchell."

She studied him with unveiled insolence.

"Listen, Barney," she said, changing her tone to one she might use in cajoling an unreasonable child. "What time was—Tommy killed?" Her voice was not so steady when she spoke.

"You ought to know," said Maguire.

"He was killed after the second act intermission, wasn't he? After everybody had left the smoking room and the washrooms downstairs except him and whoever shot him?"

"Well, what of it?"

"If I can produce a city magistrate who was sitting behind me and talking to me for five minutes before the second act curtain went up? And if he can tell you that I wasn't out of my seat until I left the theatre and you saw me in the lobby, just before the finale?"

"If you can—"

"Go to the phone and call up Dan Costello. Hand me my purse and I'll give you his phone number. He wrote it on his card for me."

"What for?"

"Inspector! What a question!"

Maguire stared at her in hostile silence.

"Of course I know," she went on, "a magistrate don't make a very good character witness these days, but Dan happens to be one of the best I could have picked out for an alibi. You'd believe him, wouldn't you? If you wouldn't, there's others above you who would. And if he won't do, I can give you the names of five or six other men, and even some women, who can testify I was in my seat all that time."

"Were you expecting to have to prove an alibi?" Maguire suggested.

"I was not. If I do say it myself, people notice me, Barney. I can name you half a dozen men who were noticing me all the time, with only one eye on the stage."

Maguire shrugged his shoulders, and began to pace the rug.

"All right, Marya," he said. "Who did kill him?"

"I don't know. Honest to God, I don't know!" Her voice rose, broke.

Nels, standing with Edwards near the door, trying to hide himself behind the big policeman and still miss nothing, somehow believed her.

"Then why did you call this number and leave that message about Jack Jordan?"

"Because Jordan was sore at Tommy, and he was coked up and I was afraid he might—" She halted.

"Might shoot him?"

"No, I didn't think that. But I was afraid he might get him. That mob of Jordan's is nothing to fool with, Barney. They'd put Tommy in the hospital for months, if they didn't beat him to death, and he'd never know who got him."

"Still looking after Tommy, were you?"

"Why not? He belonged to me."

"After what happened—"

She sat up, blazing.

"He'd of got tired of that scheming little slut quick enough. I was going to keep hands off, until he did. I was a damn' fool for raising hell the way I did at first."

"Going to play the waiting game, eh?"

"I wasn't going to play at all. I was just going to wait. He'd of come back. How do you know *she* didn't shoot him? She shot Jordan?"

"So you knew about that? Who told you?"

"They told me at the club."

"At the Del Oro? You went there when you left here?"

"Fat chance! I called up Victor. He told me."

"Victor's the manager for Jordan," Bertini put in. Maguire signaled him to stay out of the discussion.

"And then you called me up here and told me where to find Jordan?"

"Did you find him?" she asked, quickly.

"You know damn' well we found him."

"Listen, Inspector," said Marya, her eyes flashing. "If you'd be a little less of a fly cop and a little more of a friend you'd get more out of me. I want to help find the man that got Tommy, and you're throwing everything back in my teeth."

Maguire had halted almost directly over her. Now he sat down on the divan beside her, took out his cigar case.

"All right, you tell it your own way. If you didn't phone me where to find Jordan, who did?"

Czerna smiled, though her lips were trembling.

"What do you care, so long as you got him? I'll tell you this and you can tell Jordan: if I'd known where he was I'd have told you quick enough."

"It was a woman that phoned me. She tried to talk like you and she put on a wop accent."

"Why don't you take a look through Jack Jordan's address book and check up on his ex-dames?"

"We'll do that."

"It hasn't occurred to you that there might be some girl sitting in the same spot with Jordan that I was in—or you thought I was in—with Tommy? And because of the same little professional virgin of a hoofer."

"Tell me this, Marya," said Maguire, casually. "Why was Jordan chasing after Miss Paris?"

"You ought to know, Barney. Do I have to tell you the facts of life?"

"But why particularly her? Was he trying to get at Tommy through her?"

"Not if I know Jordan. He thinks he's the guy they named the Club Casanova after, or the Don Juan Club, either one."

"So you don't think there was anything else behind it?"

"There was nothing behind it except that Jack Jordan thought he could get any woman he went after, and this cutie was the next on his list. I'll hand it to her; she could get about any man she wiggled her eyes at. She's cold and calculating, but she looks hot. She might keep a man like Jordan on the hot spot, because he's just a dumb wop about women, but she couldn't keep a man like Tommy. If you want to know what I mean, I'll tell you." Her voice rose hysterically. "No man that I ever lived with is going to be satisfied with her. She don't know what it's all about. I know that type! You can have 'em! Men think they're a ball of fire, just because they've got hot lookin' hair."

Maguire patted her clenched right hand.

"Let's get back to the main point. You don't think Jordan killed Tommy?"

"I know he didn't, Barney. He was talking to me about Tommy at the club just before they called him up to the office to see this Paris. He was telling me what he'd like to do to Tommy. I told you he was coked up; it was one of the nights when Jack thought he was Napoleon. He's a Corsican, you know, and he claims to be related to Napoleon's people."

"If he was talking that way, what makes you think he didn't have Tommy rubbed out?"

"Does it stand to reason he'd shoot off his mouth about a man he'd just put on the spot? And to the man's sweetheart? Don't make me laugh, Barney! Jordan's not that kind of a fool, even when he's hopped up, or he wouldn't have lived this long."

"That's reasonable," said Maguire, meekly.

Nels had to admire the man for the way he had been working on this girl's emotions: getting her mad first and then playing dumb so she'd try to make a fool of him and spill everything she knew. Only she hadn't spilled anything that helped a bit.

The inspector took another tack.

"Have you any idea who would want to kill both Tommy and Preston?"

"Why should anybody want to kill Preston?"

"Well, somebody did, of course—"

The girl on the divan started to get to her feet, sank back, caught her bandaged ankles with her hands, grimacing with pain.

"My God, what are you telling me? Preston?"

"They took his body down to Bellevue half an hour ago. He was shot back there in his room, bent over a steamer trunk, on his knees— Didn't we tell you that when you were here before?"

She was shaking her head from side to side, unmistakable horror in her face.

"Let's see," Maguire thought aloud. "You passed out just before the fireman told us. You really fainted, then?"

"You told me Tommy was dead and you thought I faked a faint," she railed at him, her voice blurred with tears.

Maguire patted her hand.

"I'm beginning to believe now that you didn't know it until I told you," he said, soothingly.

Czerna sniffled, wiped her eyes, blew her nose. Without the heavy makeup she was even more beautiful; there wasn't a line in the ivory skin of her face and neck. Even tears and terror did not mar her.

"You have no idea who could have killed Tommy and Preston, then?" Maguire pursued.

"If I had, you wouldn't have to bother about trying him—or her," she said, brokenly. "Not if you let me get at him."

"All right, Marya. Now suppose you go in and lie down a while."

"In where?"

"In the spare bedroom, there."

"Oh my God, I couldn't!"

"All right, we'll take you next door to O'Neal's. Put her on the divan in there, will you?" he told the officer. "You'll find Mr. King in there, Louie," he told Bertini. "Ask him to come in."

"Why can't I stay?" Czerna asked, in a small voice. "I don't want to be by myself."

"You won't be by yourself. There's a detective in there watching—" he broke off. "Shane's asleep in his room."

The policeman gathered her up off the divan, gently enough.

"Now don't try to walk out on your hands, Marya," Maguire called after them. "If you'll be good, now, you'll come clear, if you've told us the truth."

"That's a break!" She tried to be gay about it and succeeded only in being so pitiful that it brought a lump into Nels' throat.

"Sit down," said Maguire to Edwards, when she was gone. "Anything you know that I don't?"

"Yes, this." The publisher handed over the letter from Twitchell and the sheets of the column copy that he had brought from the *Blade* office. He explained how he had found the letter in the early morning mail, what he had done to trace the inserted item that Twitchell had complained of and how the search had been fruitless.

"I found out where Preston went, when he went out after Tommy got here last night," he added. "Tommy sent him over to the *Blade* with the copy for the Tuesday column. We're printing it with a black border and the rules reversed."

"When did he write the Tuesday column?" Maguire asked.

"Out where he spent the week-end. He carried his portable typewriter with him."

Wylie King, his hair and dressing gown rumpled, interrupted by coming in through the door from the elevator hall, which had been left unlatched. For King's information, Edwards repeated what he had just said.

There was a long silence while King read Twitchell's letter and note, twice over.

"Did Tommy keep a carbon copy of his column?" King asked.

"Yes, I think so." Edwards got up to walk around into the office. The others followed.

The keys to the black and silver filing cabinet were hanging in the keyhole of the top drawer. Edwards thumbed through the neatly labelled folders in the top section, then started on the second.

"Here they are," he said. He took out a manila folder, marked "Column—January 1931," and laid it on the desk. Twice he went through the sheets of carbon copies; there were about a hundred of them.

"Yesterday's is not there," he announced glumly. "They're all filed in order, with Tuesday's on top. Here's Saturday's, but Monday's is missing."

Maguire went slowly through the sheets. The three or four of each day's copy were clipped together.

"Well, where would it be? His stenographer, maybe?" he suggested.

"No, Tommy wrote the columns himself. The stenographer downstairs only handled his correspondence—he used this Dictaphone for that."

"Did anyone check up the Dictaphone?" King asked. "This record's nearly used up."

"Nothing but routine business of answering his mail," Maguire answered. "Three or four of us listened to it, and there's nothing on it that we can make anything out of. We're going to take it down to headquarters along with his papers, but this Dictaphone clue stuff happens only in the movies."

Nels could feel himself blushing.

"Well, if that carbon copy's here, it'll turn up," Maguire added, scratching his bald foretop. "Probably it won't mean a thing. Anyway, the copy he turned in don't show anything had been written in on it."

"That's why I wanted to see the carbon copy," King explained. "If anybody had tampered with it, he might have forgot to destroy the original carbon."

"How do you mean tampered with it?"

"Well, if I were going to insert an item in another man's copy, I think I'd make a good job of it and copy the whole thing—or at least the page I was going to put the item on. Let's see that original a minute, Inspector."

Maguire handed it over. King studied each of the four pages. He concentrated on the second page, laid it on the desk to overlap the first page, then on the third and the partly filled fourth sheet of newsprint copy paper.

"Great oaks from little acorns grow," he said, softly. "Look here! This second page has a narrower margin on the left side, by at least the width of two letters, than any of the other three."

"What do you make from that?" Maguire asked.

"Somebody copied the second page of this and ran in an item so it would look just like the others. To make it come out even he narrowed the margin. Moreover, if I'm any judge of typewriting, the fellow that wrote this second page wasn't very sure of himself on the typewriter. He has hit wrong keys, you see, and exed out words and then typed them correctly. Tommy would have corrected the spelling with a pencil, as he's done on these other pages." The four looked at each other.

"All right, how do you explain it?" Edwards demanded. He wet his dry lips with his tongue.

King started to speak, didn't, thought again.

"Preston," he said, jerking his head toward the back room.

"But why?"

"If it's got anything to do with the murders, I'd say it was blackmail. I mean Preston was blackmailing somebody without Tommy's knowing it."

"That's preposterous, Wylie!" Edwards scoffed.

"Why preposterous? What do we know about Preston? He was an officer in the Guards. He resigned. Did you find out when, Inspector?"

"In 1921. That is, the first of January, 1922, it took effect."

"How much of a career did he have on the stage after that? Or did you—"

"We didn't find anything in his effects to show whether he had ever been an actor after that."

"An actor without a scrapbook?" King objected. "That's incredible!"

"We didn't find any—that's all I can tell you."

"Not even a scrapbook about his amateur work before he left the Guards?"

"Not any."

"Then he kept it somewhere else—unless it was burned up or lost. Once an actor, always a scrapbook keeper. Wait: did he have a safety deposit box, maybe?"

"We think so. There's a key on his ring that looks like a safe deposit key; we're pretty sure it is. But we can't find any receipt for the box rent. We'll have to send around the banks. If it's in his own name we'll find it. How about Twitchell—didn't he have safe deposit boxes? There's a couple of his keys—"

"I can give you the banks and the numbers," Edwards spoke up. "They're on file at the office, just in case something happened to him. Wylie King and I are his executors."

"I meant to ask you about that," Maguire said. "Did he leave a will?"

"Oh, yes. He made a new will last week."

"That looks like he was expecting this," Maguire suggested.

"No, I don't think so."

"Well, then, why did he make a new will?"

"To leave his property to Miss Paris."

"Oh . . . so . . . !" Maguire drew out the o's meaningly. "How much did he have to leave?"

"I don't know, exactly. Perhaps two hundred thousand, wouldn't you say, Wylie?"

"Something like that," said King, curtly.

"In stocks?"

"Sound bonds. Then there's this place; he owned it outright. It cost him about forty-two thousand."

"This apartment?"

"Yes. This part of the penthouse. Shane owns his side."

"And all of this goes to Miss Paris?"

"All of it. Tommy had no relatives living, nearer than third cousins, he told me."

"When did he tell you about the new will?"

"I witnessed it: my secretary and I."

"Who drew it up?"

"Hyman Flynn, his attorney. He hasn't been here tonight, has he?"

"Flynn's in Palm Beach," King spoke up. "I wired him after Barney first broke the news to me. He hasn't answered yet. He'll come back, though, as soon as he gets it."

"Do you suppose it would be all right to wait until he gets back here, Inspector, to get counsel for Miss Paris? In the Jordan matter, I mean," Edwards suggested.

"I don't see why not," said Maguire. "Will she want Flynn?"

"I'm sure she would want his advice."

"Well, we're not going to put her through any questioning until Wednesday, at the earliest. We want some time to get this thing organized. There's so many angles to it."

"When are you going to question the people who were named in the column?" King wanted to know.

"The Commissioner's starting on that this morning, or as early as he can get any of them in. We don't want to give 'em too much time to frame alibis. Now you boys understand that we're going to keep Miss Paris in custody and that she can't talk to anybody until she gets a lawyer?"

"Until Flynn gets here," said King. "But you're not going to put her in jail, Barney?"

"No, we'll keep her in a hotel somewhere, under guard, of course."

"She may need a doctor. And she certainly ought to have a trained nurse," King declared.

"She can have both, if somebody stands good for the bill."

"Shall I make the arrangements?"

"No, we'll have to do that. But don't worry; she'll come to no harm. I'll see to that. Now, one thing more I had marked down here to ask you, Mr. Edwards, that Wylie didn't know: who were the people Tommy stayed with over the week end—at Greenport, was it?"

"The Russell Cottinghams."

"Important people?"

"Yes, rather."

"Well, they'll be among the first the Commissioner will want to talk to. How many people were out on this house party?"

"I have no idea. Tommy just left the name and telephone number at the office. He always does that, even
when he goes to a party in New York, so that he can be
reached."

"You keep a record of his movements?"

"Yes, the desk has it in the assignment book. We can
give you the data at least as far back as the first of January,
a year ago."

Maguire made a note in his loose-leaf book.

"Now, Wylie," he said, returning the book to his pocket. "Is there anything else you think we ought to look
into?"

"As much as you can possibly get on Preston's past. I've
got a hunch the key to this may be there. Nels, where's
that list you made?"

Nels got it out of his pocket, and passed it over, not
without qualms.

"Nels was killing time over at Shane's earlier in the
evening making up his own list of suspects and questions
about the case," King explained. "Ted and I thought it
was pretty much to the point. When you put it together
with that list of the people in the column that Rorty took
down, and the one I gave you a couple of hours ago that
Ted and I made up, you've got all our ideas on the case, I
think."

The inspector was studying Nels' amateur venture into
crime analysis. The fireman felt foolish and uncomfortable. The inspector took his time.

"Can I keep this?" he asked King. King looked at Nels,
who nodded assent. He felt that his face must be crimson.
The inspector folded the two sheets, thoughtfully, and put
them in his wallet.

"Now," he said, "I've got to be getting away from here.
I've nothing to do but work on this case until we crack
it—that's the Commissioner's orders. But I want some

breakfast and a shave. Maybe you men would put on the
feed bag with me."

"No, you come to breakfast with me, downstairs,"
Wylie King demurred. "Unless you'd rather have it sent up
here."

"Thanks. You come along with me, if you want to. I
need some fresh air, before I can eat anything."

"I can use some myself," said King, getting up. "Just let
me run down to my place and get my hat and coat, and I'll
walk you around the Central Park reservoir, if you like,
Barney."

"Too far from here," Maguire objected.

"I've got to be getting back to the office," Edwards
said, without rising. "But first, if you don't mind, Inspector, I'd like to ask Wylie what he means by this suggestion
of blackmail. If I'm certain of anything in this life, I'm
certain that Tommy never even played with the idea of
blackmail."

King thrust his hands into the pockets of his dressing
gown. The right hand wouldn't go in easily. Nels suddenly recalled the picture of Preston and the girl—did Mr.
King still have it in that pocket? It was a big pocket; Nels
couldn't tell.

"I didn't suggest that Tommy was blackmailing anyone,
Ted," King replied. "But tell me why it wasn't possible for
Preston to have done it?"

Edwards blinked, pondered, said nothing. King went
on:

"Tommy complains to you that an item was inserted in
his Monday column. He says it was harmless. But once before, two months ago, the same thing happened and it was
an item on the same person. Now if Preston were blackmailing anybody wouldn't that be a good way to keep the
victim in hot water? Print something apparently harmless,
but hinting at Tommy's knowing a lot more about it than

he'd printed. There are items like that in almost every one of Tommy's columns on gossip days. It's one of the little vanities of a newspaper man—or of any gossip—to suggest that he knows a lot more than he prints. Usually he does, at that."

"I begin to follow you," said Edwards. "Go ahead."

King looked around at his audience; it was all attention.

"Tommy goes out of town for the week end. He has left the copy for the Monday column for Preston to take over to the *Blade*."

"As a matter of fact, it came by messenger," Edwards objected. "The desk told me that."

"Well, anyway, he leaves it in Preston's hands. Preston copies the second page and runs in the item he wants to insert, narrowing the margins to make it come out even. He knows Tommy won't read proof on the column this time before it goes to press. He also knows Tommy will spot the inserted item, and may raise hell about it, but he's got his bags all packed for a getaway. That means he intended to make the victim come across with cash—probably a big wad—after the Monday column was published, and then skip." He paused. "Does that make sense?"

"It certainly seems to," said Edwards, who was sitting on the edge of the divan now, leaning forward, blinking very fast.

"Go ahead," said Maguire, noncommittally.

"Preston sees to it that his victim sees the item in the paper some time during Monday. Probably he says. 'You come across with plenty this time or we'll give you the works. You've had two warnings in this column that we've got the goods on you—'"

"All right," Maguire broke in. "Grant all that. Now which of the harmless items in the column would be the ones you'd pick out to follow up first?"

Mr. King put his hand into the right-hand pocket of his dressing gown, evidently to fish out that clipping of the column he had been using all night. He couldn't get it out without first withdrawing the mounted photograph of Preston, or Captain Ruthven, and his supposed bride.

"Oh, you've still got that?" Maguire jeered at him. "Tryin' to get away with it, eh, Wylie? Let's have it, before I forget it again. Stealing the state's evidence!"

"I forgot all about it, Barney. I stuck it in there to bring it over to you. You left it on the desk when the Commissioner—"

"Yes, I recollect." Maguire put it safely into his inner coat pocket. Mr. King was now studying the column intently. Nels could hear the sound of the inspector's heavy breathing, it was so still in the room.

They waited. Maguire rubbed a hairy hand across the stubble of his beard. Mr. Edwards lighted a cigarette from the one he had been smoking. The air in Twitchell's living room—it belonged to Miss Paris, now—was stale and stifling. Nels decided to risk opening a window, but Mr. King looked up just then.

"Let me see that picture again for a minute, Barney," he said. His tone seemed to Nels to be charged with excitement.

Maguire, frowning, passed over the picture. King took it over to look at in the light from the window. He studied it a full minute.

When he turned again toward the three who were watching him, he looked at them through his schoolmaster's spectacles for several seconds before he spoke.

"Barney," he said, in a tone that seemed to be willfully casual, "I'm going to ask you to let me try something. I want to take this picture with me. I ought to be back in half an hour, at the most. I may not take that long. I wish you'd wait here for me."

"Why shouldn't I go with you?" Maguire wanted to know.

"Because if I take anybody with me, I'm afraid my hunch won't work. Even if you didn't look like a detective, Barney, just the presence of a third person—"

"All right, but where are you going?"

"I'd rather not tell."

"Don't be a damn fool, Wylie. You don't know what you might walk into. If you don't want me, there's two boys back there." He indicated with his head the room where Preston's body had been found. "They don't look like cops. Take 'em along. I won't let you go by yourself. You can leave 'em outside the place, if you like."

King shook his head.

"I go alone, or I don't go," he said.

Maguire snorted. "I never thought you were that kind of a damn' fool before." He looked at Edwards for backing.

"Let him go by himself," said the publisher, getting to his feet.

"Go ahead. But it's on your own responsibility."

King turned and walked out. As soon as the door had closed, Maguire made for the rear of the apartment. In half a minute, two men, neither of whom Nels had ever seen before, came hurrying through from the back of the penthouse and went out the front door, with only a glance at the fireman and the publisher, who were standing up now, uneasy.

Nels agreed with the inspector's claim that these two men didn't look much like detectives. He wondered if there were any more of the Homicide Squad in the back room. And what had become of Sergeant Rorty? Nels liked that fellow.

Inspector Maguire came back into the living room presently, with his collar on, his black bow tie dangling.

"Can you tie this thing for me?" he asked Edwards. "My wife always ties it when I have to put on the monkey suit."

When he had the bow about half made, Edwards asked the question that was on Nels' mind, too.

"Did you send those men to follow Wylie?"

"Sure I did. If he got shot there'd be a hell of a stink, me letting him go off by himself. They'll pick him up when he leaves the building and he'll never know he's being followed. Those boys are smart."

Edwards finished the bow expertly. "He's got to stop downstairs and get his coat and hat and overcoat."

"And his stick. Don't forget the cane. He wouldn't be caught out without it," Maguire grinned.

"A grand type, Wylie," said the publisher. "The most interesting man in New York to me."

"I hope he don't make an interesting corpse. Thank you, sir. Now that I've got to wait until that damn' fool comes back, I'm hungry as a bear, all of a sudden. How about you two?"

"It's nearly seven o'clock." Edwards returned his watch to its pocket. "I'm going to phone downstairs for some coffee. Nels, suppose you open a window. If you like, we can go out on the terrace and get some air. I recommend the view; there's not a finer one on Manhattan Island."

Gratefully, Nels went out through the office door. He paced from one parapet to another of the tower top on which the penthouse reared its peaked roof. He had lived in New York a decade and never had he seen it so glorious as on this clear, cold January morning. The rich, he reflected, certainly had done themselves a good turn when they took over the penthouse, once only a housing for elevator machinery, to live in. Nels amused himself picking out buildings he knew in Brooklyn, Queens, the Bronx, over in Jersey and up and down Manhattan Island. The inspector and Mr. Edwards, with their overcoats and hats on, were pacing around the terrace, like passengers on the promenade of a liner, careful while they were on O'Neal's side of the terrace not to disturb Miss Paris and Shane.

Nels, thinking fondly of hot coffee, decided he'd better station himself near the open terrace door so that he could hear the buzzer when the waiter arrived. He arrived just as Nels approached the doorway. Nels went in.

Not content with ringing the buzzer like a crazy man, the waiter seemed to be pounding on the metal door between the foyer and the elevator hall. Nels opened the door cautiously.

It was not the waiter. It was a small, yellow-haired, white-faced woman in a dark dress, who appeared to be stark mad.

"What is it?" Nels demanded. His voice broke her frozen terror.

"Get the police!" she babbled. "Get the police!"

She whirled and ran toward the door at the far corner of the elevator hall. As it closed behind her, she screamed. Nels raced after her.

9

Nels collided with the door as it was closing after the woman, plunged through it onto a stair landing, and ran down the concrete steps. At the landing below, the woman had gone through a door which was now closing slowly. Nels plunged after her, into a carpeted corridor. The woman was only half a dozen steps ahead of him when she disappeared through an open door.

Running through the corridor, Nels had been conscious of a battering and crashing, somewhere. As he followed the woman through the door, through

a foyer, an unlighted living room and along a corridor, he was coming nearer a terrific racket with each step. As he turned to his left into the doorway of a lighted room he collided from behind with the woman, who had halted abruptly inside the door.

He was in a bedroom, though it resounded like a boiler factory. In the corner beyond the canopied bed a man was battering at a metal door with a fire axe. The man was Wylie King, still in his wine-red dressing gown.

Nels shouted, "Mr. King!" but the little man missed never a swing with the axe. The fireman worked his way cautiously around the bed, hoping that the axe wouldn't fly out of Mr. King's inexpert hands. Once past the danger zone, Nels seized the frenzied little man's shoulder. The axe clattered crazily against the door a final time, and the fireman grabbed it on the rebound. King gave the fireman one look.

"She's in there," he shouted. The maid was screaming now in the regular cadence of hysterics. "Break it in! Break it in! Break it in!"

King jumped into the middle of the disordered bed to get out of the way.

Nels decided swiftly that Mr. King must know what he was doing. He drove two expert whacks right over the knob and the door gave inward, carrying the axe and Nels with it.

It was a bathroom he had broken into, a large and luxurious bathroom.

There was a woman on its floor.

Her head against the wall to his left, her body and legs parallel to the sunken bathtub, she lay sprawled on her back, across the deep blue Spanish tiles. Her light blue negligee was flung open; she wore under it a black, transparent nightgown and black and blue mules with gold straps. Nels studied the scene, stupidly.

Wylie King was past him and down on his knees beside the woman. Someone else collided with him as he stepped back; it was the woman who had come for help. She was sobbing and gasping, now, but not screaming. She clung to Nels.

"Phone for a doctor, quick!" King snapped. Nels plunged into the bedroom, found two telephones on the bedside table. He chose the house phone. The operator was slow to answer.

"Get a doctor up here quick!" Nels commanded. "There's a woman shot herself. Never mind—Get the doctor. . . . And don't raise the whole house. . . . All right. . . . This is Inspector Maguire speaking. . . . Snap into it!"

Inspector Maguire, with Edwards at his heels, strode into the bedroom just as Nels spoke his name, but he didn't appear to have heard it. He was making for the bathroom. When Nels got back to the bathroom doorway, Mr. King was just getting up from his knees.

"She's gone, I guess," he said, dully.

Nels, staring down at the body, could see a rivulet of blood feeling its way slowly across the blue tiles. It took him back to the basement lounge of the New Netherland Theatre, eight nightmare hours before, when he had watched just such a dark stream trickle across a tiled floor.

The dead woman was a beauty, all right. As blonde as any Norwegian girl Nels had ever seen. Silver blondes, they called them in Norway. She was a beauty from the top of her head to the soles of her feet—you couldn't mistake that, even with that queer look on her face and in her open eyes.

"What did she do—put it in her mouth?" Maguire asked, leaning over.

"Yes," said King, his breath escaping in a hiss. "Let me get out of here, will you?" He pushed past Nels and Edwards into the bedroom, raised a window.

Nels watched him uneasily. But the little man was only drawing in lungsful of the cold air.

Maguire, on his knees over the body, asked Edwards: "Where'd Wylie go?"

"Come out here, Barney," King called out. "I don't want to go back in there." His breath was still coming in great gasps. As the inspector strode into the bedroom, King let himself down into an easy chair, early American like everything else in the room. On the flat arm of this chair, face upward, lay the old photograph of the late Captain Ruthven and his dark-haired bride, and on that a dainty white handkerchief, edged with fine lace.

"What happened?" Maguire demanded, sharply. "Who is this woman?"

"Didn't you know her?" Edwards broke in, amazed. "Connie Crain."

"Who?"

"Constance Crain. The actress."

"Oh, yes! Oh, yes, I see!" But the inspector plainly didn't see.

"What made her do this?" He glared at Wylie King as though King had shot her.

"I didn't dream she'd do it," said King, between deep breaths, "or I wouldn't have let her go into the bathroom."

"But why did she do it?"

"I got a confession out of her, then she tricked me—"

"How?"

"Start at the beginning, Wylie," Edwards implored, sinking down onto the foot of the bed. His face looked a bit green.

King started slowly, still breathless from his axe work.

"I worked out this blackmail idea while I was lying down in Shane's place. When you came back with this letter from Tommy about the phony item, it convinced me my hunch was right." He drew another long breath.

"Then I had to find out which item it was. I was going through the column looking for it—and when I came to that one—"

"What did it say, again?" Maguire broke in.

"It said: 'The lofty Constance (Camera Shy) Crain was a stock ingenue in Birmingham six years ago,'" Wylie quoted, closing his eyes. "When I came to that item up there with you three, all of a sudden it came over me that the woman in the photograph looked like Connie Crain. The whole picture fell into place, like one of these crazy whirligig drawings in the films, that suddenly straighten out—"

"I know what you mean," said Maguire impatiently. "Go ahead."

"Well, the whole pattern fell into place. If Constance Crain had been an ingenue in Birmingham, England, six years ago, and this fellow Preston, or Ruthven, was an English actor, too, he could have met her. If she was the woman in the picture with him, probably he had married her. If she went out to Australia and changed her name, she must have done it to get away from him, or because of some bad scandal. If there was scandal, or she had ditched him and he turned up in New York five years later and they were still legally married, he might be blackmailing her. If he was working for Tommy, he was in a spot where blackmail was comparatively simple, so long as he could keep it from Tommy's knowledge. It was dangerous, to be sure, but this fellow was used to danger."

He paused for breath, again. The apoplectic hue of his face and neck was subsiding.

"But the woman in the picture had black hair!" Edwards objected.

"I had always thought Connie Crain's hair was too perfect to be natural," King went on. "After I'd looked at the picture again I wondered why I hadn't recognized her before. More pieces began to fit into the picture puzzle. Crain lived on the thirty-second floor, here; it was easy enough for her to go upstairs and shoot Preston without anyone's seeing her—"

"But why—"

"She had paid Preston four thousand dollars during the past six months, starting with five hundred and working up to a thousand on the first of January. It was every cent she could raise. She was rehearsing a new play, you know, for Saul Tabasco; he was going to star her for the first time." He paused for breath.

"Well, Preston demanded another five thousand before the first of February. She went to Tabasco and tried to get an advance on her salary. He said he'd give her the five thousand if she'd tell him what she wanted it for and he thought it was wise. She wouldn't tell him, of course."

"Why?"

"Because Preston, or Ruthven, was her husband. She thought he was dead, and she had married again."

"When? Who?" Edwards half rose to his feet.

"That's the one thing she wouldn't tell me. She said her husband was the finest man who'd ever come into her life, and she didn't propose to drag his name into the mud. She started getting hysterical and I changed the subject."

"But haven't you any idea?"

King looked at Edwards for a long moment.

"Not the faintest," he said. Nels felt sure the little man was lying.

"All right—we can find that out!" said the publisher.

"If he comes forward and claims her, you certainly can. Otherwise I'm not so sure. She told me she'd been married two years, and not even Saul Tabasco knew it. If his actresses marry, he's through with them, you know. If she could keep it from that shrewd old fox, the secret could die with her."

"How about the maid, here?" Edwards pursued. The woman had collapsed into a low chair over in the corner, her eyes closed, her head thrown back. She sat up now.

"If I knew his name, do you think wild 'osses would drag it out of me?" She all but spat the words at Edwards.

"Do you know it?" Maguire demanded. "I'm Inspector Maguire of the Homicide Squad," he added.

"I don't know what that is, sir," the maid said, meekly.

"He's a police inspector," Edwards told her.

"I don't know his name, Inspector." She closed her eyes and rocked her head in misery again, tears streaming down her cheeks.

"What's your name?" Maguire demanded.

"Jones, sir."

"You're Miss Crain's maid?"

"More of a companion, sir."

"How long have you been with her?"

"Six years, sir."

"In Birmingham?"

"No, sir. I took service with her in Melbourne."

"Right after she came to Australia?" King put in.

The woman's face contracted in a grimace. She was crying bitterly, now.

"Pull yourself together, and answer the questions," Maguire ordered, sharply.

The woman made a real effort to get herself under control. They waited.

"I was a hairdresser in Melbourne—a hairdresser's assistant, that is to say. Miss Crain had just come out from England to act in a touring company and she wanted her hair bleached. We'd a way of doing it—you could see for yourself it was nothing like a chemical bleach."

"Yes. Go ahead."

"I gave her the treatments. You have to have a treatment every week, or even oftener, if your hair roots grow fast. She liked me, and I liked her, and she asked me should I care to come with her on tour and be her dresser and companion like—" Her voice blurred again.

"You came to this country with her? Did you know about this husband?"

"I knew she'd had trouble in England, but I'd no idea what it was. She'd get letters at the post office addressed to Mrs. Lily Ruthven, but I never knew if her husband was dead or alive or who 'e was or whatever."

The four men looked at each other. That identified the Lily of the telephone call to Preston on Monday evening.

"When did you first know—"

A buzz, forward, interrupted. Jones got to her feet. "The door," she said.

"I'll go," said Nels.

It was the house physician, in pajamas, trousers, dressing gown and slippers.

"You're too late, Doctor," Inspector Maguire spoke up as they came into the bedroom.

Explaining matters to the doctor, after he had verified that Constance Crain was dead, took up more time. Told that the medical examiner for the police department would take over the body, the doctor prepared to go.

"I gave her a sedative about two o'clock this morning that should have kept her dead to the world until noon, at least," he said, turning away from the bathroom door, "but she was in a terrible state."

"Did she tell you what was the trouble?" Maguire asked.

"She wouldn't. She begged for something to relieve her misery. She wanted me to prescribe veronal, but I—well, in a way—" He paused. "I sensed that she was in a suicidal frame of mind. At least I wasn't going to give her any quantity of veronal. I gave her a morphia injection that was as strong as I dared administer." He turned to the maid. "How long did it last?"

"It just put her out of her head, and she tossed around something terrible. Once she got up and opened the window, and I thought she was going to throw 'erself out. I don't know how I got her back to bed. I was fair worn out, I was."

"Did you know Miss Crain was addicted to drugs?" King asked the physician.

The doctor hesitated.

"Well, yes," he said. "I had attended Miss Crain before, when her own physician was not available. Will that be all, Inspector?"

"All for the present, Doctor, thank you. We'll send for you when we want your statement—that is, the Commissioner will."

The doctor bowed himself out.

"Now tell us what happened yesterday, Miss Jones," Maguire resumed.

"Mrs. Jones, sir."

"You're married too?"

"Widow, sir. My husband is buried in Melbourne."

"It's always well to know that," said Maguire, no humor apparent in his face or voice.

"It is, sir. If Miss Constance—"

"You were going to tell us what happened yesterday. Did you know Miss Crain was being blackmailed?"

"I only suspected it, sir."

"How long had you suspected it?"

"Only last week."

"How? What made you suspect it?"

"It was my evening out, and I went to a cinema, sir, and I felt faint and came home before half after nine o'clock. I'd a bilious headache coming on. I came in unexpected, and found Miss Constance in this room, here, with this Mr. Preston."

"You knew Preston, then?"

"To be sure I did, sir. There's not a girl in this building that didn't know Mr. Preston."

"Popular among the ladies, eh?"

"Oh, no, sir. He'd have nothing to do with us. The 'andsomest man, but you'd think he was a royal duke, the way he kept to himself."

"You're from London, aren't you, Jones?" Wylie King put in.

She ignored him.

"Answer the question, please," Maguire ordered.

"I was. My 'usband and I both. We went out to Australia the year 'e come home from the Rhineland."

"You never saw or heard of Captain Ruthven—that was Preston's real name, you know—in London, then?" King pursued.

"Never until I saw him here."

"You're sure of that?"

"Oh, yes, sir." She made her answers to the inspector, ignoring King. Maguire asked the next question:

"You didn't see him or know anything of him in Australia? Now tell the truth; you're not going to come to any harm if you tell the truth."

"No, sir, and it's God's truth I told you," she flared up. "I never saw Mr. Preston under any name until we moved in when this apartment was finished. Last January, it was."

"You had no idea he had any connection with Miss Crain until last week. What made you suspect it then?" King asked.

"Because she 'ad been crying. Her eyes was swollen 'alf shut, that night. She sent me straight to my room. I heard him leave by the service door, and then she came in and gave me what for. She said I was spyin' on her. And I don't know which of us was in the worst state after that was over. But she believed me, I'm sure—that I'd come home ill and—"

"Why did you connect Preston with her husband?" Maguire prompted.

"Well, I keep an eye on her check book, unbeknownst to her. I've done it right along since I've been with her, just to make sure how things stood. She was a highly impulsive young lady, if you understand me, sir. Three or four times I'd saved her a good trimming. She would take a drop too much and sign checks she'd no business giving. Once it was twelve hundred dollars. After that mishap, the bank was instructed not to honor checks to unknown parties without consulting Mr. Tabasco's office. They looked after her like a child, that way."

"Then how did she get the money she paid Preston—or that she told me she paid him?" King wanted to know. "About four thousand dollars in all, in sums of five hundred to a thousand over the past two months."

"Not out of her banking account," Jones replied directly to King for the first time. "She'd only eleven hundred on hand before Christmas, and she was down to a few hundreds lately. Of course the play was opening out of town next week, and she could always draw an extra advance from Mr. Tabasco while a play was running."

"She was drawing ahead on her pay?" Maguire put in.

"She always did. It's quite the regular thing in the theatre."

King verified that. "Women and most men for that matter, who are working under contract the way Crain was, are generally in hock to the management.

Particularly women of Connie Crain's type; money slipped right through her fingers."

"You knew she spent money on drugs? It must have been a good deal," Maguire suggested.

Mrs. Jones nodded. "What a pity!" she said, wiping her eyes. "But the drugs didn't cost her so much, considering. She dealt with honest people. She wasn't a fiend—not yet."

"Where did she get this money she paid Preston, if she did pay him that much?" King interposed.

"I'd suspect she got it from Miss Starling. Understand me, sir, I don't know that," Jones qualified, hastily. "I shouldn't want Miss Starling to—"

"Who is Miss Starling?" Maguire asked.

"Her best friend. It was through Miss Starling she came to the States. Miss Starling was in Australia and saw Miss Constance work. She wrote Mr. Tabasco and brought Miss Constance to the States and Mr. Tabasco tried her and gave her a contract for five years."

"I happen to know that's correct," King put in. "That's Susan Starling, the actress."

"Is Miss Starling also addicted to drugs?" Maguire asked.

"How should I know, sir?" Jones resented the question.

"Positively not," said King. "She was frantic when she found out about Constance. I know she got Crain to go to a sanitarium and take a cure last summer. It was my understanding that she was cured."

"I think she was," Jones spoke up, "until this trouble started."

"Then you think Miss Crain borrowed this money—the four thousand dollars—from Miss Starling?" Maguire resumed.

"I don't know where else she'd 'ave got it."

"When did you next see Preston and Miss Crain together—after that night in this room?"

"Never again."

"Do you think she saw him again before last night?"

"How should I know, sir? I know she was about out of her head on last Saturday. She'd got a telephone call and she sent me out of the room. And when I came in again she was lying face down on the bed, and that white you'd 'ave taken her for dead." She shuddered at the ominous word.

"Go ahead."

"Well, she took a dose of something and she slept, fitful, through Sunday night. Monday she had a ten o'clock forenoon rehearsal and then a fitting at the costumers' and she came home at three o'clock in the afternoon. She was trembling all over, the poor thing. She'd a page she'd torn from this terrible newspaper, the *Blade,* I believe it's called, and there's a man writes a lot of stinkin' scandal in it of the name of Twitchell. He lives in this building; Mr. Preston's his sec't'ry. I've seen him; he looks like a decent gentleman, and you'd never believe he'd write—"

"You were saying," Maguire interrupted, "that she came home with a page torn from the *Blade.*"

"She did, sir. She collapsed on her bed and I asked what could the matter be and she went into regular hysterics. I picked up the paper after she was quiet and took it to my room. But all I could find on it about her was something about her being in stock in Birmingham six years past. Thinks I, now I've got it; she saw that piece and it brought back the past, the poor thing—"

"What did you do with the paper—the one you picked up?"

"It's in my room. Shall I get it?"

"Not now. Go on."

"After a time she got up and sent me to the pantry to make tea. I was worried about her, so I stood just outside in the corridor after I'd put on the kettle. I heard her ring up Miss Starling, but she couldn't get her; Miss Starling was still at the theatre, they said."

"What time was that?" King wanted to know.

"About five o'clock."

"What then?"

"She kept ringing Miss Starling every half hour or so, until half after seven, and then Miss Starling's maid telephoned she'd left word to ask Miss Crain to come see her at the theatre after the first act. I took the message. So Miss Constance told me to telephone to the box office and get her a single seat if I could. There was one, and she sent me over to get it."

"When was that?"

"It was eight o'clock when I got to the box office, and twenty after when I got back here."

"Why should she have sent you after the ticket?" Edwards asked. "The box office would have held it for her."

"Well, she said she wasn't sure when she'd get to the theatre, and she did want to see some of Miss Starling's show. The poor thing, I thought to myself, she won't know what it's about if she sees it. But she put on her new evening dress—the black and silver one. At half past eight, she went out, though the performance wasn't to begin until ten minutes of nine and likely not until after nine, being a first night. Well, it hadn't been ten minutes she was gone when a gentleman rang up and I answered and he said: 'Lily?' and I thought he'd the wrong number and I asked what number he wanted and he said 'What number is this?' and I said 'This is a private telephone,' and he said 'Are you Miss Crain's maid?' and I told him I was her companion and he said, 'Very well, tell her that Winnie called and said to call him at once.' He was most emphatic about it. An English gentleman, by the short way he talked to me. I told him she was out, and he said: 'See here, you'd better find her and tell her I shan't wait all night.' I said: 'But she's gone to the theatre, sir,' and he said: 'Well, go after her, and deliver my message. She'll thank you for it. Just tell her Winnie called and says he won't wait all night.'"

She looked around at the four intent faces.

"Go on," said Maguire. "What did you do?"

"I don't know why I should have done it, taking orders from a strange gentleman, but I put on my hat and my fur coat and went. It was twenty past nine when I got there, though I took the subway at Fifty-seventh Street and rode down to Times Square. I had to buy standing room to get in, and it took me a time to find Miss Constance; she was in a seat that was beyond a pillar so she couldn't be seen from where I was standing. Finally I had to ask the head usher if Miss Crain was in the house and she asked the other girls and one of them knew where she was. I should have remembered the stall number from the ticket, but all I could remember was it was in row H."

"Wait a minute," Wylie King cut in. "That seat was on the right aisle, just at the corner of the box, and to the right of a balcony pillar—a single seat, I mean, with the pillar shutting it off from the rest of the row."

"How did you know, sir?"

King looked around the circle.

"I sat in the same seat, later," he said, "and picked up this handkerchief with her initial on it. When I showed her the handkerchief, here, she broke down and confessed—and I was just bluffing—but go on."

"Well, I waited until the first act was over, and I stopped Miss Constance as she was coming up the aisle and I whispered to her about the gentleman calling and just what he said, and she said: 'Do you know what he meant, Edith?' and I said I hadn't the faintest notion, but somehow he had made it sound like life and death, and she smiled queer like and she said: 'It is, one or the other,' and then she said: 'Edith, you're to sit in my seat from now until the end of the show, unless I come back.'" She paused, dabbing at her eyes.

"Did you sit in her seat?" King prompted her.

"I did through the second act, but I was so fretted about her I couldn't keep my mind on the play though I must say Miss Starling was magnificent. When Miss Constance didn't come back for the third act, I just couldn't sit still any longer, so I went out into the foyer and asked the manager if he knew where Miss Crain was, and he said 'Yes, I saw her go into the New Netherland across the street when the crowd was going back in after intermission.'"

Maguire interrupted: "What was that, again?"

King explained it: "The Wilde show was so long that its intermission ended at the same time as the intermission after the second act across the street at the Nichols. I noticed that. The *Rebel Rose* intermission was nearly half an hour long, you know. Go ahead, Mrs. Jones."

"I walked across after her. The doorman asked for my check but I swept by 'im."

"What was your idea in going over there?"

"I wanted to keep an eye on her. She was actin' queerer than I ever saw her act. Wild, like. I was all goose flesh, Inspector."

"Did you find her over there—at the New Netherland?"

"I never did. There was such a terrible crowd, and so many standing in the promenade, and when I'd try to look down the aisles an usher would say. 'I am sorry, madame, but you cannot stand in the aisle.' So I gave it up. I went downstairs into the ladies' room to telephone here and see if she had come home, perhaps. But there was no answer."

"You had no change," Maguire put in, "and you got the colored maid to change a quarter for you and you gave her a ten-cent tip when you came out of the booth. You had been crying."

"Good heavens, sir! How did you know?"

"If I had only stopped you as you went upstairs, I'd have solved this case in jig time, probably. But I let you get by."

"Why should you have stopped me, sir?"

"With a dead man in the booth down there— But, how could we know you had any connection—"

Jones leaned forward, tense.

"What dead man?"

"He was in one of the booths under the stairway."

She put a hand over her lips. "Who, sir?"

"Twitchell, of course."

She looked blank. "You mean him?" she jerked a thumb toward the floor above.

"Who else?"

"An 'eart stroke, was it?"

"Are you trying to be funny?" Maguire snapped.

"Indeed no, sir. My husband died of a stroke. Not in a telephone booth. In the bath, it was."

"Are you trying to make me believe you didn't know Twitchell was killed?"

"Indeed I didn't sir. Though I can't say I'm sorry, after what he—"

"Haven't you seen the newspapers? Where have you been all this time?"

"Right here, sir. I came straight home from the theatre and waited up for Miss Constance—"

"When did she come in?"

"At a couple of minutes past midnight. She was out of breath, as though she'd been running, and I think she was out of her right mind. She had something under her coat— She pushed past me into this bedroom and locked the door. And I had to threaten to call for help before she'd let me in."

"What then?"

"I got her undressed and in bed. She was cold all over, and out of her head and no mistake. She was muttering things and cursing, horrible, under her breath. Then, of a sudden, she sat up and said: 'Edith, give me the pistol!' I didn't know about any pistol, and I told her I didn't, soothing like. 'It's in the bathroom,' she said. 'Bring it to me.' I went into the bath and made believe to look around, but of course there was no pistol in there."

King sighed heavily. "Of course, there was," he said. "If there hadn't been—but why be sentimental?—it was the best way out for her."

"You mean the pistol was in the bath, all the while?" Jones demanded.

"Where else? I know she didn't have it when she went in there; there were no pockets in her dressing gown and she had on nothing else but that transparent nightgown."

"But where was it hidden, sir? I thought I looked—"

"In the clothes hamper, under the soiled linen," King cut her short. "Didn't you notice the linen is all tumbled out on the floor. What next?"

"She got up and went into the bath. I went with her, though, and I wouldn't leave her, though she tried to put me out and raged at me and talked something terrible. Finally I got her back into bed. I'd a terrible time; I do think she was quite insane at the time. At two o'clock I slipped out long enough to send word down by the lift operator to send a doctor. She was some quieter after he came, but I 'aven't been ten feet from her since then until this man came—"

She looked at King and began to weep again.

"Did you send her out of the room?" Maguire asked King. "While you talked—"

"No, Miss Crain sent her out. Jones looked at me, and I nodded for her to go."

"What I wanted to tell 'im," Jones put in, bitterly, "was not to let 'er get at no pistol nor window nor nothing in the bath so she could do away with herself—" She buried her face in her hands.

"Don't have that on your conscience, girl," said Ted Edwards, gently. "Providence moves in mysterious ways . . ."

"And who might you be, sir?" Jones asked, looking up, her face streaming with tears.

"I'm the publisher of— I'm a newspaper editor," Edwards amended. Jones fixed him with her weak blue eyes.

"A fine one you are to talk about conscience. If it—"

Maguire held up an authoritative hand.

"Take it easy, sister. Now, Mr. King," he indicated the bathroom with a motion of his head, "Did she tell you what happened at the theatre; how she shot Twitchell?"

"Yes, she did. She went to Sue Starling during the first intermission and tried to borrow five thousand dollars more. Sue just didn't have it to lend her. Sue tried to find out what she wanted it for, and Crain couldn't bring herself to tell her that she had been lying to her about her whole past life for years. Starling was just too dear a friend and trusted here too completely, she said. Sue's maid was working on her and couldn't be sent out of the room. Well, she sat in Starling's dressing room all through the second act, trying to make up her mind to tell Sue the truth, but she couldn't. Then she got the idea of going across the street, finding Twitchell and either bluffing him or throwing herself on his mercy, telling him she simply couldn't get the money for a couple of weeks and not five thousand dollars at a time then."

He paused to assemble his story. "I'm putting this thing in chronological order. As I got it from her it was all jumbled up, part of it hysterical.

"She found Tommy in the lobby and asked him to see her downstairs in the lounge. I suppose her face convinced him that it was important; anyway he joined her there just as the last stragglers were going upstairs for the second act. They sat down on a divan in the smoking room. She said he pretended not to know what she was talking about and tried to tell her that he had never seen the item until he read it in the column. She blew up and told him not to insult her by trying to make her believe anything as flimsy as that. Then he told her he had written a note of protest to Mr. Edwards about the item and would get Edwards on the telephone and prove it. He went around to the booths under the stairs on the men's side and she followed him. He couldn't get Edwards either at home or at the *Blade* because, as he knew, Edwards was upstairs seeing the show. There's no doubt that Tommy thought she was out of her right mind and was just humoring her.

"Well, she told him, standing there in front of the telephone booth, that he'd better take off the false face and talk business; that she couldn't pay him five thousand dollars at any time, that she couldn't keep on paying such big sums. Then she pulled the pistol out of her bag and said something to the effect that he'd kill the goose that was laying the golden eggs if he didn't watch out."

"What did she mean by that, exactly?" Maguire asked, frowning.

"She'd been carrying this pistol since Saturday, meaning to shoot herself if there was no other way out—or so she told me. She thought maybe she could show Twitchell how desperate she was by telling him that and showing him the gun. Then he wanted to know what in hell she meant by this talk about paying him. We know, of course, that he must have been astonished and puzzled by what she was saying. But to this poor woman it meant merely that Twitchell was not only blackmailing her but was trying to deny it. She just went haywire, then. She could remember his grabbing at the pistol and feeling the recoil and hearing the shot; seeing the flash, smelling powder. He fell back into the open telephone booth; the stool caught him and held him in a sitting position. She expected somebody to come running, but nobody did. She could see, then, that she'd shot him through the head and that he was already unconscious. So she propped him up in the booth so he'd look as though he were waiting on a telephone call, and closed the door on him. As she did, she noticed that clipping of the column—the page she had torn from the *Blade*—sticking out from under the door of the booth. She grabbed at it, and it tore in two. She started to open the booth door to get out the piece that was jammed under it, but just then she thought she heard someone coming down the stairs, so she beat it into the woman's side of the lounge. A man did come downstairs and go into the men's room. She walked up the stairs while he was in there."

"That must have been me," Nels spoke up. He, too, had been that near catching the murderer, red-handed.

"Why on earth did she leave the torn paper—a perfect clue?" Edwards demanded.

King answered him. "She wasn't thinking of that. She just wadded up the piece in her hand and threw it at the Chinese jar as she passed, and it hit the floor where Nels found it. That's my idea."

"I see," said Edwards. "Go ahead."

"Well, she walked all the way home from the theatre, planning what she would do. She'd left Jones in her seat in the theatre; they're both light blondes. She might prove an alibi that way; Jones would tell any lie for her. If Ruthven were only out of the way, she'd never be suspected. So she came up to this floor in the elevator, walked up the stairs to the penthouse, went in under the pretense that she was going to pay Preston—or Ruthven—the five thousand, and then shot him while he was getting her letters out of the trunk."

"How did she know she was getting all the letters?" Edwards demanded.

"She didn't. She should have stayed and made a methodical search for any clues that would point to her. She had been buying back pictures, clippings, or a scrap book each time she paid her husband an installment of the blackmail. But with Twitchell probably dead or dying over in the theatre, do you wonder that she couldn't stay in there and make the search? She grabbed and ran."

"Where are the letters she got?" Maguire asked.

"She destroyed them last night, while she had Jones locked out of this room. Sent them down the sewer and then, and not until then, she remembered leaving the torn column in the booth. She didn't remember what she'd done with the piece that came away in her hand. It was worry over that clue that made her so frantic, as Jones had told you."

"Well, gentlemen," said Inspector Maguire, rising and walking to the bathroom door to look in. "Once again I've got to call in the medical examiner. And I hope to God it will be the last time on this case."

The four others got to their feet.

Maguire was haggard and blue-jowled in the sunlight streaming in through the east windows. "When I have phoned," he said, "let's eat breakfast. You'll have to tell all this over again to the commissioner, Wylie, when we go down to see him. Is there anything else you can think of now?"

"I just thought of one thing," said King. "Ted, do you happen to know the name of the play that Connie Crain was rehearsing?"

"No, I don't recall it."

"The play," Wylie King paused and looked around his four auditors, building up his dramatic effect, "is called *Tell and Be Shot!*"

Imagine that ten months have passed. Imagine that you are up in one of the drab streets of the Hunt's Point district of the Borough of the Bronx, whose brick, steel and stone hives shelter more human bees than swarm on Manhattan Island. It is half past four of a morning in next December; raw, wet, cold, a northeaster blowing.

A policeman with a nightstick is leaning against the brick wall of a warehouse in this mean street. Inside the black rubber raincoat, beneath the cap covered with the same funereal composition, glistening under an arc light, are a figure and a face that must by this time be familiar to you. For a policeman who has that morning attended a wedding—the wedding of his friends Shane O'Neal and Patricia Paris, he appears to be much too gloomy.

It is Patrolman Nels Lundberg. Nels has been through the policeman's training school, with colors flying. He knows that after fourteen months more of this pavement pounding, if the administration is not changed, he will be promoted to detective third class, as a reward for his work on the Twitchell-Ruthven-Crain case.

At the moment, however, he is not contemplating the delights of being a real detective in a metropolis of crime.

He is thinking how snug he would be back in the firehouse of Engine Company No. 21, with a good detective story to read, a nice, warm bed, and no alarms until morning.

MURDER
AT GLEN ATHOL

NORMAN LIPPINCOTT

A strange clan—a grotesque dinner party—and
violent death in a little Pennsylvania town!

MURDER
AT THE
KENTUCKY
DERBY

CHARLES PARMER

MURDER ENDS
THE SONG

ALFRED MEYERS

3 DETECTIVES
MURDER
ON THE RAILS

WHITECHURCH · THORNE
· TORGERSON

Coachwhip Publications

CoachwhipBooks.com

THE STUDIO
MURDER MYSTERY
THE EDINGTONS

SMOKE
SCREEN

Lawrence Saunders

THE SEVEN BLACK
CHESSMEN
John Huntingdon

DEAD
WEIGHT
ADDISON
SIMMONS

Coachwhip Publications

CoachwhipBooks.com

MURDER A LA MODE

ELEANORE KELLY SELLARS

CLASSIC RED BADGE PRIZE MYSTERY

MURDER ON THE BLUFF

ESTHER TYLER

MURDER BY JURY

MURDER ON THE APHRODITE

RUTH BURR SANBORN

MARIAN GALLAGHER SCOTT

DEAD HANDS REACHING

DEATH'S LONG SHADOW

Coachwhip Publications

CoachwhipBooks.com

ALIAS FOR DEATH

BARBARA LEONARD REYNOLDS

THERE IS NO RETURN

THE ADELAIDE ADAMS MYSTERIES

ANITA BLACKMON

ODDS-ON MURDER

DANCE

JACK DOLPH

FEAR CAME FIRST

VERA KELSEY

Coachwhip Publications

CoachwhipBooks.com

ORCHIDS
TO MURDER

HULBERT
FOOTNER

The Perfumed
Death

MADELON ST. DENIS

The
MURDERS AT HILLSIDE

VIRGINIA
RATH

NO FACE TO
MURDER
EDITH HOWIE

Coachwhip Publications
CoachwhipBooks.com

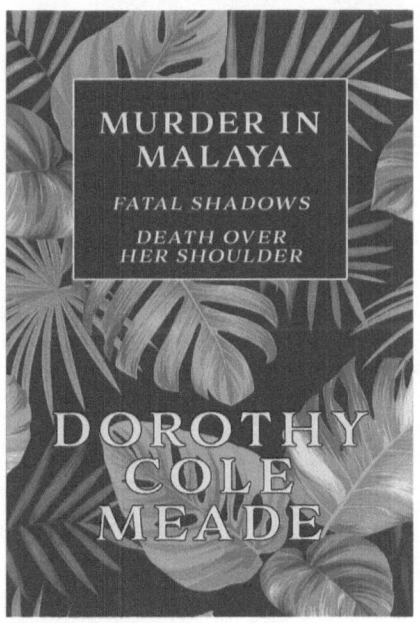

Coachwhip Publications

CoachwhipBooks.com

NOVEMBER
JOE

DETECTIVE OF THE WOODS

H. HESKETH-PRICHARD

MURDER
IN A WALLED TOWN
KATHERINE WOODS

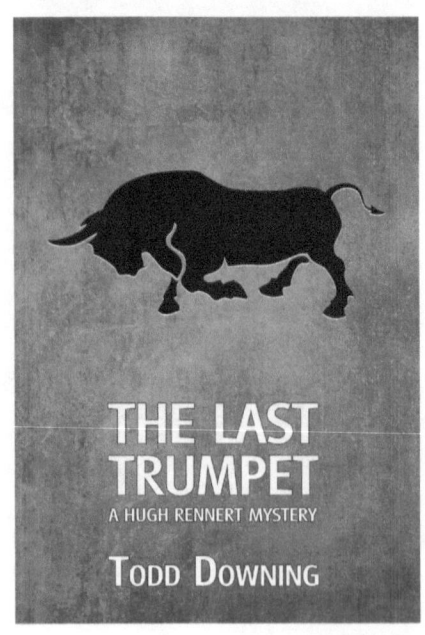

THE LAST
TRUMPET
A HUGH RENNERT MYSTERY

TODD DOWNING

DEATH SAILS
THE NILE
F. BURKS MCKINLEY

Coachwhip Publications

CoachwhipBooks.com

FEAR OF FEAR

FLORENCE RYERSON
COLIN CLEMENTS

MURDER IN THE FAMILY

NICE PEOPLE MURDER

Mary Hastings Bradley

3 DETECTIVES
FEMMES AUDACIEUSES
MERWIN • SOMERVILLE • FOOTNER

DEATH DOWN EAST

Eleanor Blake

Coachwhip Publications

CoachwhipBooks.com

THE FIRES AT
FITCH'S FOLLY

KENNETH WHIPPLE

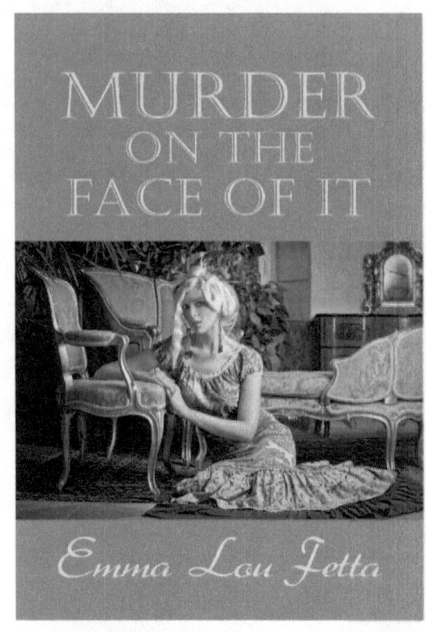

MURDER
ON THE
FACE OF IT

Emma Lou Fetta

GRIMM
DEATH

THE
GROUSE
MOOR
MURDER

JOHN FERGUSON

Coachwhip Publications

CoachwhipBooks.com

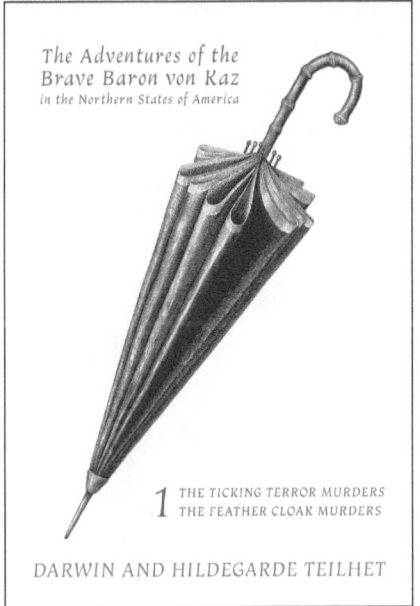

Coachwhip Publications

CoachwhipBooks.com